To Jemi
All the k8t,
Mike
15/4/23

3

Like Water

With the heat, a vapour rising,
With the chill, a frozen icing,
With the mild, a river flowing,
With the rain, a world is growing.

With the heat, a passion rising,
With the chill, a soul is hiding,
With the mild, a life well-lived,
With the rain, a life to give.

Part One – Life

It was the time of life.

It was the time of death.

It was every moment of every hour.

It was all the time that time could give.

Nothing would persist of those first days.

No traces.

No half-recalled glimpses from which a past is fashioned.

No means by which the surge and the touch of the river could return to the present, resurrected from the wells of memory.

The canvas was empty. These days were that tight sheet, stretched over a frame, soon to be masked by the accumulated brushstrokes of a life cast out of its home, thrown across the seas and brought back again. Of a life cloven in two by chance and circumstance, rendered into pieces by the whip hand of nature. Of a life lived under the weight of love tasted and unfulfilled, of suffering and forbearance in the face of hardship. Of a life in which faith would wane and ebb and stretch thin, in which the gods of the sea and the air and the land, gods without

voice or sight or mind, would test the fabric from which that faith was woven, press apart the fibres that form the whole, those strands singular, which alone offer little, but which entwined can hold the weight of all creation on their backs.

These were the days of which there would be no trace.

It was the time of life.

It was the time of death.

*   *   *

Every second swirled, thousands of impressions marking themselves on the senses like raindrops darkening the surface of a pavement, disappearing as soon as they hit, their shape leaving the world forever, replaced by the deepening hues of the stone pathway. Those impressions dispersed themselves from staccato events in the course of time and turned into the unrecoverable foundations of all that would make up the heroine of our tale, of all that would become Freda Salmon.

Shrouded markers of awakening. The passage between not and is.

Emerging from the start, from her beginning, seeing herself for the first time in the glinting eye of a brother fish, Freda became aware of the world into which nature's hand had thrust her. And so too did the awareness of her own form rise inside; of herself, whole and alive; of heat and shape and sound; of all that was her.

What did she know of this place in which she swam? What did she know of these waters, of their pulsing rhythms and changing shapes? What did she know of the river and its world?

As days gave up their light, and darkness swarmed the sky; as the glow of orange branches eased apart night's curtains; as white clouds slipped in front of the sun; as time passed and the water and the land and the heavens danced the dance of time immemorial; as all this remarkable, unremarkable, silent, noisy spectacle conducted itself without interest or indifference, Freda Salmon came to know that she was alive.

Life fell upon her slowly at first. It had been there since the day of her birth – it had been there forever before she floated forth and it would be there forever in the endless days that afterwards would come – but the time that was hers, the time in which she moved and breathed, swam and fell, played and loved: that was the time in which life, total and complete, made itself hers.

Freda Salmon felt something unnameable deep inside her silvered form. It spoke in faint whispers, in murmurs and vibrations, in flits of feeling, in momentary flushes of absolute certainty, in brief washes of faith, warm and comforting.

She felt life inside of her, an energy popping and crackling between the edges of her soul and her body, binding the two together. Making a whole where once there had been only disparate parts.

She could not name it. She could not speak of it – for who can talk of that with no name? And she could not fix it when she came to look, when she tried to hold what she knew was there.

It shifted and changed shape, ran away from the inner eye as she turned to catch sight, trying to fasten the mystery onto some spot in time and space.

But no matter.

No matter to Freda Salmon, who knew it was there. Who felt it and willed it and believed in it.

Some observers might say that those things unknown and unseen cannot exist. Some might say that Freda Salmon simply believed in her own belief; that she brought forth an illusion in which a reflection of herself floated, unchanging and still; that she reimagined the world as something other than what it was. Some might say that she was too accepting, too prepared to yield to the first truth that made itself known to her.

No matter.

No matter to Freda Salmon, who knew of the life that sparked inside her veins. Of the life that drove her to be.

Of the life that bounced and ran and spun and flew inside her. That was always there, in motion, moving and changing, flashing this way and that, always travelling, always alive.

In the days that followed those first few, the sparks took Freda Salmon from the dusty bed of the river up into the near reaches of its illumined body.

Here she came to know that she was not alone.

The water teemed with tiny salmon the same shape and size as her. Now and then, bigger fish joined them, dispersing the quick-growing infants. Sending them back to the protective cover of the riverbed.

Food was abundant. The hungry salmon, desperately seeking to grow, feasted on everything they could find. Sometimes spoils were shared. Sometimes a single fish would fight off all others and gorge on whatever it had won for itself.

At first, Freda took her time. The food left from her birth, provided by the mother who had died before she was born, conveyed through the egg in which she had rested and grown in the months before life fully became her, provided a safety net in which she could rest.

And then, after watching the sleek movements of her kin, so many of whom would fall by the wayside, as they availed themselves in myriad manner of the river's harvest, she thrust herself forward and joined them.

Flashes of silken flesh, like living mirrors, darted left and right, up and down, sped across her eye-line, dropped and rose behind her tail. They cast diagonal trails, zigzags, spirals. The water was a blaze of orange and brown and silver. Tiny eddies swirled and died. Jet streams lagged behind their creators, quickly fizzing away, leaving only a few dissolving bubbles floating upwards into nothing.

For a moment she hovered, tail shaking back and forth. Unseeing fish knocked against her, jarring her out of her space. She felt herself roll to one side, lose balance, fall.

Convulsions rippled through her body. Muscles wrenched and pulled. She was away, moving among the mass, eyes flitting, senses ringing loudly as the information of her new surroundings engulfed her.

The distance gone, the safety of the bottom removed, her whole body tingled and ached with the complete immersion in a new world, a universe that connected to the one she had watched from the riverbed in the same way the faltering dregs of an echo connect to the first vital bellow of the lungs.

She moved without control, embedded in the flow.

Thousands of fish slashed and scored their way through the water. Jets and wakes and trails crossed and died, rose in clock-ticks of violent uproar, and were brutally dismembered by the driving effervescence of young lives making themselves known in the world.

Freda lurched to one side, saw an onrushing group of embryonic salmon and threw herself toward the river's floor.

Her body resisted, groaning beneath the unfamiliar speed and jerk. She felt a spasm across her scales: brief, stretching pain experienced for the first time, a marker staking out the edge of her range, laying down the boundary of potential her body held in these early days.

The group moved on, a shadow passing between her and the light.

Blood pulsed. Her heart hammered. Her mind shot ahead, careering about in the unlabelled sensations gleaned from her first foray into the river proper.

She looked up, tried to focus on something.

A gap ran to the surface. She could see a shape: large, outstretched, a water-tinted mixture of brown and green.

She kept her eyes fixed on the tree's form. The dust of the river's belly was close. She was almost lying on top of it.

In the space above her, the fish continued to act out their feeding dance. As they raced and dipped and shimmied across her line of sight, she held firm, focussing her energy on the spot she had chosen, willing herself to calm.

Slowly, ever so slowly, her shape grew looser. The tension faded from her sides, her fin, her tail. It faded like the imprint of a kettle's steam on the cool glass of the kitchen window.

In the small cavity of her chest the blood slowed. Each beat came a little later, pulsed with a lessening force.

Across the contours of her mind images and noises, tastes and impressions resolved themselves into connections and memories, hardened into familiar shapes, settled upon the canvas.

Her tail fell still.

The unbroken line cast from her glistening eyes quivered and broke.

A kick.

A flash.

A whip and a flex and she was among it again, surging through the crowd, dipping and spinning, scoring left and right.

Her mouth cracked into a wide smile. A bubble-edged yelp of delight escaped into the current.

The water, the swarm, the river sang in her ears. They sang the songs of the species, of the world; sang the songs of all that was and is and will be; sang them in full voice, firm and strong.

Freda Salmon felt the voices. She heard them. She sensed them.

She moved and she moved, consumed by the mass, liberated from it, with the river and against it, floating on the voices of the flow and the forefathers and the fire, then kicking and flashing against them, swirling them into new rhythms and sounds.

And before she knew it a chorus had formed. The was and the is and the will be climbed together in creative destruction, clashing and colliding in fierce bursts of energy. Neither side could cease. Neither could cede. Neither could forgo the moment in favour of the other.

Nothing could permit it. Everything demanded they met and met and met again, spiralling upwards with and against each other, interwoven strings of past and present and potential.

Freda threw herself onwards. One moment she was of the mass, clinging to her senses amid the onslaught of the shared mind, the next she was leading them herself, carving out new pathways within the river's flow.

She held and held, straining as the opposing forces spun against each other, discordant and discomfiting.

The spaces in front of her tightened. The river was breathing in, pulling the edges of the world closer together.

And then it came.

Bursting forth from the outer limit of all that was bearable there was harmony. It filled every space, infiltrated every drop of water, saturated the entirety of Freda's body and soul. The old and the new bound in choral song, a union of voices lifting up the world and casting it anew, subsuming, reforming.

And Freda knew she was alive, as she had known from those first few moments. But this knowledge grew and expanded. It entwined itself among her muscles, her flanks, her fins. It slid across the surface of her scales and penetrated to the recesses of her mind.

She was truly a part of the river now. A part of something completely; and certain of that communion.

The past was less than what it had felt when lived.

In the glassy rush of the river, Freda broke the roof of the mass, pressed toward the surface, stopped and turned.

Below her she saw herself, first in the thousand echoes of her kin, second in the eyes and the faces of those nearest to her, who looked and reflected, naming her as she named them: not entirely, not in total, not with the suffocating pull of the net, but partially, enough, leaving space in which to breathe and to be.

High above the water birds glided on warm currents. Below, in the space beneath the river's boundary, Freda Salmon cast aside the first flush of youth and joined her brothers and sisters in the search for the future.

*   *   *

Time passed. The school thinned. Those who remained grew fat on the river's fare.

Freda Salmon staked a home for herself. She talked and swam with the other fish. Her name played across their lips and so too did she speak theirs. The river provided for them, as their parents had known it would. As it had nourished them in their own youth. And so too their parents before them, in times now long distant and all but forgotten.

On occasion, fish of different territories would break the invisible boundaries and enter the homes of other groups.

One such salmon made himself known to Freda in the faint light of the early morning.

'What's your name?' he asked, swimming slowly through the lightening river.

'Freda,' she said, 'I'm Freda.'

'Nice to meet you, Freda,' he replied, 'I'm Jacob. Are you coming?'

He whipped his body round, buzzed his tail in front of her, sashaying a stream of bubbles into her eyes, and darted upwards, towards the surface.

Momentarily dazed, Freda pushed through the fizzing disruption and flicked her head toward the light.

Jacob was waiting, tail moving from side to side. As she caught his eye he smiled and then dropped through the translucent water, righting himself as he reached the line on which she was resting, still uncertain as she shook off the residue of surprise.

He held his form, waiting for her.

Freda looked on, her body briefly, imperceptibly tautening, ready for speed.

Jacob cocked his head to one side and smiled.

Freda reciprocated.

But before her lips could crack into the full valley of fellowship and recognition, he was off, tail slashing through the river, jets and eddies trailing in his wake, as if the water had been laced with a pearl string of gun powder, set alight by the silver-shimmer of his sides, undercut by the scent, the eye-echo, of hot, fire-encrusted orange.

And in less than a moment Freda was following, moving without restraint, the patterns of routine flung to one side.

She flew through the water, crashing in and out of the quivering streams Jacob carved into the river.

He flashed a look back, saw her in close pursuit. A grin broke across his face, mirrored in the jawline of his accomplice.

The two friends, for that was what they had become, shot and dived, arced and pinwheeled, chased and led. Two fireflies bound in flight as the sunlight bleeds its final red strips of heat across the shortening canvas.

Up and down the river they raced, rising and falling in long, lung-drawn breaths, battling against the water's current, gliding and tumbling along the unending charge of the river's flow.

They broke in and out of groups of fellow fish, cutting channels and rivulets through the loosely thronged shoals, thin slices of absence that cleaved into view as Jacob pressed his way between the silver-orange affiliations, that remained as Freda followed, as the dispersed allies shimmied and jigsawed away from the pair of speeding friends, and that closed up like enfolding flowers, casting all space outside of themselves, denying any trace of the path that had been so swiftly cut.

Freda gained speed. She overtook Jacob, buzzing a trail of frothing water in front of him.

He let out a giggle, burst through the swirl and pursued his companion. Freda fired off, flying first to the surface then diving towards the bottom.

She fell through the river, swift and bright and silken, fell and fell with all the force of the water driving through her, hastening her body towards the floor. And Jacob fell, only a handclap behind, chasing, smiling and laughing, and calling after her, his words muffled by the river's swell and the roar of speed.

The hard brown bed reared up at them.

Freda flicked her tail.

Her face passed within a fin-slash of the floor as she bent her body and surfed across the river's flow, slinging herself upwards.

Fast, fast she flew, her body spearing through the surge.

Jacob followed. He caught the movement of her tail, read her intentions. With a muscular wrench he fired himself in pursuit, started to gain ground as they raced through the water.

He was an inch behind. Then closer. Then closer still, almost touching her tail, propelled by his greater bulk and the crackling delight popping and bursting inside his chest.

Pushing and pushing he strained against the water, strained against the limits of his body.

And they were side by side, quickening towards the river's edge.

And they were sprinting, travelling with such speed. Speed they had never known before. Speed of mind, speed of body. In and out of the river they sped, in and out of each other.

Together they flew, surfing across the rip and the flash of the current. Up and up, hurtling in liquid arcs of unbroken bend and whip, crashing through the streaming water, searching for each other and themselves. Pressing back the boundaries of life in budding communion, diving forward, heads first, flushed and excited, ignorant of what was there, electrified by the prospect of discovery, enchantment, with the river, with the world, with each other.

Two friends, momentarily as one, journeying together, bound by the gently woven strips of care and affection blossoming between them, which erupted into fuller and fuller life as each second passed.

And then the water ended, and they rushed beyond the confines of their world.

The two of them soared. Soared into the sharp, cool air of the morning, shocking themselves as they breached the barrier of all they knew, as they felt the surface of their scales prickle and dance, neither of them aware of the dark echoes of pain and endurance this leap of joy and surprise and hope hesitatingly, tentatively foretold.

For now, the future was a place which had no hold. All that existed was the here and now, shooting out in every direction. These heartbeats of exhilaration were the complete and total experience of all that was and would forever be.

They remained in this perpetual present as they re-entered the water, gilded by the leap they had taken. Unknowing of what awaited. Unaware of the hard paths of life etched into the days long hence. In their minds, they felt the firm hand of certainty renewing the faith they had in the world, felt the beginnings of faith in each other, saw the wellspring draw closer as they journeyed onwards, saw themselves reaching their fins towards the source.

And in those origins of faith and hope and belief, they saw the future, saw it reimagined and retold as the endless, joyful reprising of those first, wonderful moments. Of friendship and love. Of all these things found and marked, given and received. Of life, lived and living.

*   *   *

The sun rose. The sun fell.

The passage of the days was marked.

Freda and Jacob grew; so too did their kin; so too did the river, buoyed by rains and melt water.

Not all could endure. Disease and scarcity shortened the days of some. Chance and fate cast their flickering nets across the paths of others.

Maturity called to those who remained, speaking in saltwater echoes of shared memory. The voices of the sea sang in soft harmonies deep inside the salmon of the river. They cooed of shoals and space, hummed the sounds of the brine, played across the inner senses in brief, strong pulls, casting strange yet familiar longings into freshwater minds.

Something stirred inside Freda Salmon.

It ran beneath the surface like a drum slow-tapping in the basement of a house.

She could not name it; she could hardly even speak of it.

But it called inside her, quiet and resolved. Not once did it seem that it would cease.

She could taste it in the back regions of her tongue. The knowledge that only the sating of the instinct would return the balance she had once enjoyed.

Gradually, her mind changed. Decisions altered. The low rhythm of the sea increased its influence, extending into every corner of her life. It was an inheritance bequeathed to all the salmon, felt by every one of them.

Between her and Jacob there grew an understanding, never spoken, never named. It occupied the space that lay amid them both, that bound them, more tightly than before.

A journey awaited.

The life they had built for themselves was approaching its end.

Throughout the river, in salmon large and small, similar feelings grew. Bodies moved slickly; eyes darted; fins swished and whirled.

Everything was imbued with the unspoken tension that creeps across us all in times of deep preparation; the kind of provision that has little to do with the body; the kind that claws and scrapes at the sunken trunks, long overlooked, in the dark, neglected alcoves of the mind.

It was a time of danger for Freda. So too for Jacob. So too for every fish whose inheritance bestowed on them the call of the sea.

$*$ $*$ $*$

'When do you think we'll move?' asked Freda in the dark of the evening, the sun lying far below the horizon, the creatures of the river slipping in and out of sleep.

'Soon,' said Jacob, 'I'm sure it will be soon.'

Freda shook her head.

'How can you be sure? There's no signal, no one to tell us. What if we go at the wrong time? What if something happens?'

Jacob swished his tail, swam in a short circle around Freda and came to rest beside her, his head nestling against hers.

'We just have to hold firm. When the time is right, we'll know.'

His voice faded as he spoke. His gaze floated away from her, downstream, along the flow of the current. The river looked back at him, bleak and shadowed.

'I just wish it could start, that's all. This waiting … it's making everybody tense. I can feel it in the water. The way other fish are moving. Their faces. Their eyes … so anxious. I can feel it as well … inside me. It's like a sound I can't quite hear, but I know it's there. Can you feel it, Jacob? Is it changing you as well?'

He looked at her, waited as the shadow fell from his eyes.

'I feel it. I've felt it for weeks, months. It's like it's always been there. Always.' He paused, sighed. 'I can't remember what it feels like for it not to be there.'

Silence.

They moved closer together.

Side by side, polished skin touching, they rested.

'I think it will be alright,' said Freda, after a few minutes. 'I think it will be like the time we leapt, only harder and longer. But I think if we're together then we can do anything, go anywhere. We'll keep each other safe.'

'I think that too,' said Jacob.

Next morning, a great buzz of expectancy suffused the water. Energy fizzed through the river in a way not seen for as long as most could remember. Fish moved erratically, travelling in strange patterns devoid of the sense and certainty that usually characterised their activities. Groups of salmon formed and separated. Fish who did not know one another fell into deep conversations before parting with sudden jerks of the tail.

'Do you think this is it?'

'I'm not sure,' replied Freda. 'It could be.'

She looked around, saw movement and evasion.

'Or maybe it's a false alarm. Everyone is so tense. Fish act without thinking. They're doing things they wouldn't normally do.'

She looked at Jacob.

'It wouldn't take much for someone to get spooked.'

'Or to do something stupid,' he replied, staring ahead, trying to identify some kind of design within the random movements.

They remained as they were, in the space where they had slept, close to the riverbed. Pods continued to form, debate, then disperse.

'Let's go up there,' said Jacob, 'find out what's going on.'

'Why don't we wait a few minutes more? See if it resolves itself into anything.'

'I don't know if it's worth waiting any longer. They might be talking about setting off. We don't want to get caught and have to catch onto the back of everyone else.'

'No,' said Freda, 'of course we don't. I just think we could hold off for a moment – try to get a better sense of things. Maybe we wait a little longer. What do you think?'

Before Jacob could reply a large male salmon broke out of a dissipating pod some feet in front. With a heavy swish of his tail the water behind him erupted and he was travelling toward the pair.

'Have you heard?'

'Heard what?' said Freda, as she and Jacob watched the large salmon approach.

'The news. Have you heard the news? What are you going to do?'

'What news?'

'You haven't heard, have you?'

'No,' said Freda, 'we haven't. Who are you?'

'Leith,' said the fish tersely, 'but that isn't important.'

'Well, I'm Freda and this is Jacob.'

'Fine, fine,' said Leith. 'But what I want to know is what you're doing?'

He swam up and then down again, flicked his head from side to side, made to move away, stopped and waited in front of them.

'Well? What are you doing?'

'But you didn't tell us the news,' said Freda. 'You didn't say what it was we had to decide.'

'You said you hadn't heard, didn't you?' The question was accusatory in tone. 'Well, I'll tell you then, and you can tell me what you're going to do.'

'Come on Leith, spit it out,' said Jacob, nipping towards the large fish and then back to Freda's side.

'It's going round that a group of salmon have decided today is the day. They say they're fed up with waiting.

When the sun passes its peak, they're going to start. That's what I'm hearing, anyway. They're going to set off for the sea.'

Freda's eyes widened, the muscles along her flank contracted.

Jacob swam in a short circle. He drew closer to Leith.

'Who told you this? Who said it? Was it one of the ones in this so-called group? What are their names?'

'Some fish, that's all. Doesn't matter who it was. I didn't know her and she didn't know me. What difference does it make? Everybody knows what's happening and everybody's got to make a choice. Are you going with them or not?'

Freda was looking beyond Leith, into the body of the river. His words redrew the map of what she saw. Labels and signs fluttered into existence. Where before there had been nothing, now she could discern meaning and pattern and purpose. The whole of the river was deciding. Everyone was trying to find out what was happening, who was going, if the thing was true.

And did it matter if it was true or not?

'How do you know it's not a rumour?' said Jacob. 'Things have been tense – really wound up, you know? What if this is just a bit of sand whipped up into the swell?'

'And what if it isn't?' said Leith, staring back, his eyes still.

'Maybe we should go up there, Jacob, see what we can find out.'

'I haven't got time for this,' said Leith, 'are you two going to go or are you going to stay? What does it matter if it's true or not? If enough fish believe it, then it's the truth. And I tell you what, as far as I can make out, there are plenty of fish up there who believe today's the day. No question.'

'Never mind us,' said Jacob, his voice rising and his fins spreading out. 'Make up your own mind instead of trying to get other people to do it for you.'

Leith's eyes narrowed.

'Forget you then,' he said, 'I'll find out what other fish are doing. Should never have bothered swimming over here in the first place.'

He slapped his tail through the water and swam off. Bubbles flashed in his wake. Freda and Jacob felt them buzzing across their faces. As the fizz cleared, they saw him disappearing into the excited throng.

Freda nudged Jacob.

'Does it matter if it's true?' she said to him, her words gentle yet firm, animated by a growing resolve.

Jacob turned to look at her, his fins still spread, the brief billow of antagonism not yet blown out.

She held his gaze; watched as the remains of his anger left him.

'Does it matter? If they believe it, they'll go.' She flicked her head as she spoke, signalling the swarm above. 'Maybe half of them are looking for an excuse. I mean, we don't even know what it'll feel like when the time is right, do we? Maybe we'll never know. Maybe we'll just have to go; put our faith in the river and the sea.'

Jacob looked away.

'It's funny, isn't it?' he said.

'What's funny?'

'Belief. Sometimes you have it and sometimes you look and look but nothing's there.'

Freda buzzed her tail against his, kindling the memory of their first meeting.

'I guess that's when you have to take the leap,' she said.

An old silence fell between them. The silence that comes when it is known the words to follow will do things: cleave, join, marry.

'I will if you will,' she said, her heart quickening inside her chest.

'And so will I,' said Jacob, his own heart beating faster.

For a brief moment silence returned. It was a pause in which resolution sprung up, in which the kernel of faith made itself known once more, climbing slowly, fitfully from beneath the rubble of recent times.

'And so we'll go,' said Freda, controlling her breath, feeling her blood hot beneath her skin, nudging the side of her body against Jacob's, tracing her fin along his silvered frame. 'We'll make the leap.'

Part Two – Journey

The sun was high.

Beneath, the river flowed quickly. Water slapped and splashed and spat along its course, compelled toward the sea, however long that journey might take. And all this from nothing but a trickle high up in the mountains. A gentle stream from which creatures took their fill, bathing and drinking in calm shallows cooled by alpine air; from which plants slaked their thirst; from which the occasional climber would fill their bottle before moving on, in search of the peak.

As the mountain gave way to forest the stream grew thicker, widening through soft soil. Over countless years it had carved a path, tinkering at the edges with every rush and push of ceaseless movement.

Only the speed and volume altered. Rains and melt water increasing both. Heat and drought lessening the river's power.

Across the long, dark reaches of time, creeping back beyond the words and minds of women and men, beyond even the inheritance of the river's progeny, the salmon and their ilk, there was the water's birth: the first broken steps that signalled the spluttering into life of the channel that one day would come to dominate the land – a benign ruler whose dominion extends from the shadows of the tall, hard mountain bodies, across the splayed out shelves of green and brown, and on to the salt-licked edges of the land.

Cycles could have been discerned within those ancient years, had any conscious mind been there to see them. Cycles of feast and famine; of burst banks and rapid, violent torrents racing towards the saltwater, charging through forest and across grassland like a fleet of horses stampeding down a canyon; of deadening absence in which the passage that fell from the heights to the sea looked like a faded memory of something once grand but now forgotten, corroded by time's acidic hand.

And then there had been the deep freezes. The periods in which cold and ice gripped the land like a vice, choking it into submission with slow turns of the handle, tightening its hold until all but the quietest of life's beasts were silenced, and so too the voice of the river.

But what of now? What of the time in which Freda and Jacob found themselves? What of the days and months and years surrounding the lives of these two young salmon, of their kin and of the others who shared their world with them?

This was a time of plenty. A long, low cycle of fluctuating temperature, rainfall and sun, one in which the polarities remained distant. The changes that came never travelled close to the extremes the river had had cause to know.

All things were in abundance. Not every creature may have felt this richness, for how could they judge if abundance was all they had known? But all revelled in it, knowingly or not. Species prospered, territories expanded and competition lost the bitter, ravenous edge that poisons the senses like sulphur lying heavy in the air.

In the forests, across the fields and meadows, over the untamed lowlands, mammals and birds and insects took from the river all that they needed. Within the confines of its shifting boundary, the great flow of water provided for fish and for others, for creatures smaller than anything accessible to human eyes, of liquid, of night, of zip and stretch and climb.

Despite the great bounty of the river, the salted cry of the sea still rang in the minds and the bellies of the salmon. Still called to them with words and sounds of power and control. Still summoned them, a destiny pulling at the ties that bind, urging their owners away from the safe and the familiar, from the comfort of routine and repetition, from the expectation of a world static and unchanging, echoed in the habits and customs of life lived in recurrence, again and again, day after day.

Yet this was not the only call that travelled along the river.

For we must ask the question: where does a river's boundary cease?

Is it at the edge of the water, rubbing up against the mud and the sand of the bank?

Is it past the bank, at the point where the flow no longer sustains the lives of those creatures who hang close?

Or is it at the tips of the branches of the trees standing nearby? Those trees in which the eagles perch, watching and waiting for the signs of movement their sharpened eyes and whetted claws long to see.

A second call was travelling along the river.

High-pitched whistles rose and fell.

Changes imperceptible to the eyes of most tapped against feathered primal memories, rousing them from sleep.

Positions changed.

Wings unfolded. They beat in hard, strong arcs.

Pushed hungry bodies into the skies.

Yellow, sharp-bladed eyes moved in their sockets, eating up the world below, drinking in the impressions that bled through the river's surface.

Waiting.

*   *   *

'Are they moving?'

'What, up there?'

'Yes, yes. Are they moving? They look like they're moving.'

'It isn't time though. He said it was after the sun reached its peak. Look,' Jacob pointed his body toward the sky, 'it still has a while to go. They can't be moving yet.'

'They are. They're moving. Over there. Look, Jacob. There must be hundreds of them.'

'What? They can't be going. Hey! Hey! What are you doing? It isn't time yet!'

His words were lost in the water. The group of salmon were already too far away to hear him.

'We've got to go, Freda. We've got to go now. They'll leave us behind.'

Panic fringed his words. He buzzed around, swished his tail, moved forward then back, fins flapping without decision.

'Wait,' said Freda. 'What about those?'

She took hold of his fin and gently turned him to look up into the river's body, at an area behind the group who were moving. There, they could see a second mass of salmon. These were stationary.

'Why aren't they going?' asked Jacob, his eyes uncertain, his lips mouthing further, unvoiced questions.

'I don't know,' she replied.

Jacob looked downriver.

'I think they're gaining speed.'

'A split's not good for any of us,' said Freda. 'Numbers are safer. It won't be good at all. Everybody knows that. Everybody knows numbers are important. Why would they split up?'

'We have to decide, Freda. We need to decide. If we wait, there won't be a choice,' said Jacob, swaying from side to side; his body jerking towards the unmoving group and then off in the direction of the travellers.

The salmon who remained showed no signs of movement. A couple of fish left the pack and hung in the water a few feet in front, staring after their kin.

With a swift flick of the tail they were back among the group, swallowed up by the mass and sharing what they had seen.

'It's this atmosphere,' said Freda. 'The tension. It's been building and building. Now it's snapped. They can't take it anymore. It's split them. Us. They couldn't take any more of it, that's why they've left. Rumours, truths. Who knows? They just couldn't take it.'

Jacob stretched his fin out and took hold of Freda's.

'This is it then,' he said. 'We'll have to choose. What do you want to do?'

She looked up. Saw the group who remained, saw the group who had left.

Her breath was short. She clenched her teeth, felt pressure growing behind her eyes.

'Safety in numbers,' she said. 'Everybody knows that.'

She turned, looked at Jacob, moved towards him, kissed him.

'Let's go,' she said. 'Let's go.'

*   *   *

Two bullets tore through the river, slicing the liquid apart, carving shimmering paths out of the depths, the water sparkling and glinting underneath the late-morning sun.

Neither of them had moved with such speed before, not even on the day they first leapt beyond the confines of their world. Entwined with the current, they flew forwards faster than the flow itself.

Freda could feel the force of the water all around her. At once it was in front and behind, beneath and above, threatening to consume her, to wrench sovereignty from out of her grasp.

With all her body she clung on, pressing herself towards the mass of fish ahead; the edge of her fins scrabbling to maintain a hold, struggling to keep control of her line and her balance.

Bits of grit and silt and rock assailed her, flung up by the water's flux. Crashing into her sides and face they felt like sharp teeth needling her skin. Her eyes stung. Her tail ached.

Pushing her head up she caught sight of the group. 'Yes,' she thought 'we're gaining on them.' The words raced around, careered off familiar tracks and smashed into a wall, collapsing into fragments and dust.

Everything was fixated on the group. All her energy and effort and senses were at the limits of her capacity. She knew if they did not reach the travellers, then danger would stalk the two of them all the way to the salt – if they even managed on their own to follow the fin-slashes of their forebears into the beckoning sea.

She willed herself on. Willed and willed and willed her bones and her scales and her fins, every part of her growing body, sitting now as it was on the cusp of adulthood. This was the last cry of youth, reckless and all-consumed, absolutely certain in its mission, in its momentary abandonment of everything outside of the goal, the single desire that called like a Siren, mesmerising, demanding to be sated.

Freda flung herself across the surface of the current, slinging her body along the cusp of the water's press.

They were nearing. Singular salmon began to appear ahead. She could just make out individual fish, her eyes straining to see through the tumult.

The mass gained in size, crystallising into familiar shapes and forms.

With a cry of pain and triumph she gave all she had left to the river.

Control dissolved into the current.

Her body took over as her mind collapsed under the weight of the race.

Nothing was hers anymore.

Hurtling through the flow she absolved herself, withdrew all ownership, passed it on to momentum and to speed and to force.

Her fins flattened against her sides. Water shot across her scales, waves of liquid whipping along every part of her body. She flew; like an arrow she flew, still accelerating, still gaining on the travellers.

A small piece of decaying shell dislodged from the riverbed. The water grabbed it, threw it upwards.

Freda saw it leave the bed, glimpsed, for a moment, the sharp, jagged edges spinning in the current, remnants of a creature long passed.

She jerked out a fin, tried to steer herself to one side.

A sharp, hot stinging sensation cut through her mind. She steeled herself, tensed her body.

Pain called out from all over, submerging her senses. She willed it to stop. Jumped on top of it. Beat it down with her fins.

It continued to call, unrelenting. She pulled her muscles tighter, felt her sides aching beneath the force of her effort.

She released her grip on herself and screamed. It was in her tail; a deep throbbing soreness pulsing up through the whole of her body.

She could not stop. The group were there. They were in front of her. Inches away. She could not think, could not reason with herself. This was the chance. Safety in numbers. She had to make it. They couldn't do it alone.

Another scream whistled from her lips as the water whipped across her back, as it threw her tail hard to one side.

How close was it now? Her eyes were stinging. She could feel a white pall gathering pace, falling across her sight. She blinked, thrust her head forward, blinked again.

The pall disintegrated.

Swishing tails came into view, beside her.

She pushed, one last time, almost spent, gasping for oxygen; she pushed.

And she was among them.

*   *   *

Inside the school there was space to breathe. Travelling together meant a split workload and Freda was able to glide in the slipstream of a larger fish towards the centre of the group.

Gradually her composure returned. The pain from her tail still called but not as loudly as it had. Muscles burned across her sides, smouldering with the heat of lactic acid. The disparate thoughts and sensations clamouring for her attention died down, replaced by relief.

She sighed; a deep, long sigh. A sigh of thankfulness but one in which the sadness of departure also rang.

Cries were bouncing through the shoal. Fish were swimming towards the surface and looking behind the group, momentarily losing contact with the mass before dipping back down and reattaching themselves.

Freda tried to tune into what was being said. The sounds ricocheted around, eluding her as she moved.

And then the remains of the reverie that had enfolded her in the hot, flushed seconds after making contact were shaken off, the pain from her tail silenced and the newly minted relief drained away.

What of Jacob?

Where was he?

At the start of the pursuit, they had been together. She'd assumed it had remained that way, that she could sense him by her side as they scored their line through the river. And then in the torrent of movement and desperation that preceded their – or was it just her? – catching of the school, all that she was had been given over to the chase and the last, frantic bridging of the gap.

'Jacob!' she shouted, 'Jacob!'

Around her salmon turned and looked.

'Who's Jacob?'

'Jake? Do you want Jake?'

'What's wrong, friend? Did you leave someone behind? We had to go you know. There wasn't any way of convincing the others.'

She flew upwards, eyes darting, head twisting, slashed back down through the shoal, cast looks in all directions, desperately trying to pick Jacob out from the fish surrounding her.

Nothing.

She called again, repeating his name, hoping for a response.

Nothing.

And then, out of the corner of her eye, she saw another fish leave the top of the pack and stop, briefly, above the throng, to look back upriver.

Blood rasped through her veins; her heart returned to the manic pump it had been in the moments before she caught the school.

Expelling all notions of fatigue, she bent her body and shot through the roof of the shoal. She spun round and looked behind, into the river's swell.

There, some metres away, struggling to make up the ground, was a salmon. Solitary. Alone.

She dipped into the pack, regained their speed and passed through the roof again.

Buffeted by the flow of the water she rocked from side to side, trying to see if it was Jacob.

Again, she had to fall back into the school; again, she had to rejoin them, feeding off their momentum to recover her pace.

Once more she left the top of the pod. This time the salmon was closer, the gap a little narrower.

There was a break in the current but still Freda could not be sure.

She looked down. The group had slowed slightly, marrying their pace to the fluctuations in the river's flow.

She dived into the rear of the pack. Confused fish furrowed away from her, throwing up shouts and protestations.

Ignoring them she pushed her way to the very edge of the shoal and looked out across the void.

It was him.

It was Jacob, his face contorted, his whole body struggling, trying to make up the gap.

She flashed round, whipping her body through one hundred and eighty degrees. The school threatened to escape her, but she clung on, flapped her fins and clawed her way back to the far boundary of the group.

The eyes of those either side lay upon her, narrow and disapproving.

She did not care. These brothers and sisters of hers were not of consequence, not now, not in these desperate seconds.

A jolt ran through her body as she cast out both her fins, flattened her tail sideways. Immediately she lost momentum, juddering almost to halt. Fish whizzed past, shooting across her eye-line, escaping her. Aching and pained she wrenched her fins and tail backwards in one single movement, sending her body forwards just in time to catch hold of the very edge of the shoal.

She was hanging onto the tail of the group, swimming solo in the conjoined slipstream of the salmon.

Flicking her head for a moment she could make out Jacob's shape. He was close; she could feel that he was close.

'Jacob!' she called. 'Jacob!'

No response.

He had to be close. He must be. Safety in numbers. Two not one.

She called again, tried to time her shout with the brief flick of the head she could allow herself if she wasn't to lose touch completely with the school.

Absence.

No voice made itself known to her. No sign came across the shortened space.

'Keep going,' she thought, begging the river and the noise and the force of the water's flow to help her. 'Keep going, Jacob.'

Then she heard it.

A stifled yell, indistinct, familiar.

She flicked her head again, held it for a fraction longer.

He was so close now. She called to him, called harder this time, a stream of bubbles spraying out of her mouth.

Another sound. Louder, nearer.

A shout, nervous and eager.

He'd recognised her, she was sure of it. He knew it was her. He had to have recognised her. He had to keep going.

Freda stared into the shoal. Concentrating everything she had left on the swimming fish, sucking the last drops of energy from the far corners of her flesh, she began to reel herself backwards.

In tiny increments she decreased her speed, maintaining a check on the others as she did.

She was abseiling over the edge of a cliff. The slipstream and her vision of the group were the ropes connecting her to safety.

Slashing through the water she fought to keep herself in between Jacob and the shoal. The throb of her tail called angrily as it felt the brunt of the current. Pain pulsed up her body, across her back, through her fins, banging at the doors of her mind, threatening to enter, to rampage into the space and deny everything that remained there.

The water smashed against her, tried to pull her away from the group.

Muscles groaned and stretched. For a moment she lost sight of the school. Panic rose like hot steam. She shook her head, jarring it to either side. The salmon returned, lost only in a brief kick-back of bubbles.

Time was short. She knew it, tasted it. Her energy was waning. Something had to be kept. She still needed to make the gap. It could not all be used in waiting.

'Jacob! Jacob!'

One last time she called.

No reply.

Noisy silence. The rush and push and press of the water shouting in her ears, specked with no other sounds, cut apart by no voice, no cry of recognition.

Still the pain, still riding through her.

Remnants now. The fleeting remains of what she could give.

It was over. She had to go back. Had to fire herself into the shoal with what little persisted.

'Freda.'

A voice, close and weak.

She turned her head, saw him beside her, felt his body brush against hers.

Jacob.

'Come on!' she yelled, 'We're nearly there. One last push.'

Scraping the walls of their reserves, scavenging the near-empty floors, pulling scraps and flecks from the desiccated surfaces of ossified relics, Freda and Jacob threw themselves across the void, sailing beside one another through the smooth, fast water of the slipstream.

They reached the shoal. Buried themselves deep in its centre.

Dark and protective the mass swarmed around them, encased them in silver and orange and brown. Jacob gasped and spluttered. Freda steadied herself, clamped down on the pain consuming her body, denied it an audience as she reached out and touched her fin onto Jacob's skin.

'Made it,' she said. 'We made it.'

*   *   *

Night hung heavy across the land. Those creatures who lived by darkness commuted across their territories. Intermittent noises broke the spell of the shadows.

In the river, the shoal rested out of sight, down in the bowels of the flow, amid thick slivers of green and brown clumped together on the bed, swaying slowly in the current.

Here the river was more powerful. It held the land in its fist. Broader and deeper than in the place Freda and Jacob had once called home, it was a liquid chasm sunk into the surface of the earth; a great gash slicing through rock and soil.

The group were at rest, Stillness wrapped its comforting arms around them, guiding the salmon to sleep.

Freda, though, could not remove herself from the succession of events.

Beside her, weakened by the chase, Jacob drifted in and out of consciousness, his body calling him to rest, while his mind glowed hot from the charred embers of that day's desperate drive along the river.

With tired eyes Freda watched him enter and leave their world. Since the fevered moments in which they hurled themselves back into the shoal hardly a word had crossed their lips. The few they had exchanged were dwarfed by the exhausted silence and gentle touching that had done their speaking for them.

Now, catching Jacob in a moment of awareness, Freda murmured softly to him, her voice slow and mild, mirroring the movements of the river.

She asked him how he was, where he hurt; asked him of all that she could see in him but not feel for herself.

He replied in halting sentences, fractured and split, broken up by long, heavy breaths.

She soothed him with comforting words glossing together the consequences of the battle they had won; with visions of hope and plenty cast from the abundance of the sea's rich bounty; with recollections of simpler times, when they had known innocence as a world total and complete, rather than as a memory increasingly distant.

And as his breathing slowed and the tension in his body seeped away, she asked how it had happened, how the two of them had become separated and alone. But there she stopped, for she knew the despair that had swept across her in those anxious moments was not for now, that it would burn and sting the both of them.

Jacob's head bowed under the weight of the questions. He felt the anger return. The fear and the desperation. Those same emotions that had coursed through him as he raged against the current, that had whipped him into a flurry of misery and guilt as he had tried to catch the shoal.

After a time, he began to speak.

He explained how he had followed her from the bed of the river, how he had remained behind, keeping her in his sights along with the school. Then he talked of turning a first time to look upon those they had left. He had wanted to see them, hoping they would have begun to follow.

On they had travelled and then a second time he had looked, the remaining salmon now fading into the distance, shrinking away in the soft, familiar waters of their shared origin. A little further and he had taken a final, sorrowful look. A last chance to see their kin. But as he had turned his head to face the future, he felt something strike him hard on the base of his body.

What it was he did not know – a stone, a rock, a shell perhaps. It hit him at speed; he was unbalanced from turning, rocking offline because of the change in his body shape. It slapped him into a spin, sent him careering across the river, his body whirling through the flow.

He had managed to right himself before hitting the mud wall of the bank but, by the time he had shaken away the shock and re-set his line, Freda was gone and with her the shoal as well.

His voice waned and the story bled out to nothing.

Nestling up against him, touching his fin with her own, Freda called Jacob to sleep, her voice bending and shaping itself around him, wrapping him in her words. He slept deeply, she in patches, the pain in her tail rising and falling through the night.

*   *   *

Messages swam through the shoal, instructions and plans for the day ahead. Freda was awake. She listened as first one and then another fish told her what was intended.

She woke Jacob and together they set about readying themselves. They took a little food where they could find it and inspected each other's wounds. Freda splayed her fins across Jacob's underside while he, in turn, attended to her tail and revealed to her the extent of the damage.

Matters were not as grim as she had anticipated. There was a small tear at the tip, but the wound was clean and looked like it would mend quickly. The pain would stay for a while, Jacob suggested, but it was likely to die down over the next few days as her body healed itself.

When the signal went up for the group to move off it came as a release for both of them. There was much to leave behind and little they needed to take forward now they were together again.

For two days they continued along the water's path, the shoal moving swiftly and without interruption as the river grew wider and deeper. They meandered past tree-lined banks, flew down small waterfalls and drops, crashing through the spray before rejoining the foaming current and darting on.

Salt beckoned them. Whether the sensation was real or illusory, none could say. But all believed they could taste faint specks of the sea fusing with the fresh water.

At night they hid in the shadows of the river's belly, finding places to rest, veiled from the eyes of predators.

By day, the safety of numbers and the serenity of their progress saw a sense of camaraderie develop, one distinct from the loose bonds of kinship and affiliation that had characterised the entire, unbroken school back in the higher reaches of the river.

The salmon were growing. With each advance downstream, youth fell further behind them. They were shedding the skin of their early days and, from beneath it, emerging renewed.

Friendships blossomed. Words and laughter rippled through the shoal.

Talk was of the sea, of the salt, of the great adventure that lay before them.

*   *   *

On the morning after their ordeal, Freda and Jacob found themselves swimming alongside a trio of fish, one of whom they recognised.

At first Leith was nonplussed by their greetings, protesting that he did not know them, had not met them and, as if to prove the point, was completely ignorant of their names. But after they cajoled his memory, needling it with light humour at what had once felt so urgent, a smile broke out across the large, powerful line of his jaw.

'Of course I remember you!' he exclaimed, dipping and rising in a short dance of excitement. 'I didn't think you were going to come. Thought you'd end up staying behind with the other lot.'

They told him about the chase and how close they had been to separation in the alien waters of the river.

He and his companions listened, eyes glinting as the story reached its climax, though by tacit agreement the two of them had stripped away its darker moments.

'Well, I'm glad you made it,' Leith said. 'It's like I always say, there's safety in numbers. And you two seem like a good couple of fish, as it goes.'

Leith's friends, Elu and Lox, introduced themselves. They echoed Leith's thoughts and spoke in eager voice about the story of the chase.

The five shared much over the two days. They talked of the past, how naïve they had all been, and the future, imagining the possibilities that awaited them. From time to time, they exchanged a few words about the present, the changing shape of the river and its surroundings, the cycle of the skies and the progress of the pod, who pressed forwards with purpose.

On the morning of the third day, Freda woke to find Leith and Lox talking to each other a little way off from her. Their tails buzzed through the water and their fins moved quickly.

Elu and Jacob, back from hunting for food, joined her.

'We thought we'd leave you to sleep,' said Jacob. 'Looked like you needed a rest.'

'Is your tail still giving you pain?' asked Elu.

'It's not so bad, now. I think today will probably be the first day where I don't really notice it.'

Jacob smiled, held Freda's gaze and then moved away from the two of them so he could peer across at Lox and Leith.

'What do you think those two are talking about?'

He nipped back to where he had been, his eyes slightly narrowed.

'I don't know. Any ideas, Elu?'

'Beats me,' she said, shrugging her fins.

They saw Leith leave the conversation and come towards them. Lox followed a few lengths behind.

Leith's face was flushed, his eyes bright and alert. Stopping in front of them he executed a roll, tipping his whole frame over on its axis before blowing a stream of bubbles up towards the surface as he righted himself.

'This is it,' he said. 'That's what they're saying.'

'What's it?' asked Freda, her eyes held by Leith's gaze.

'The sea,' he said. 'Destiny.'

Part Three – The Sea

Freda and Jacob swam through the water's form, feeding on the river's bounty. In each other they saw reflections of the changes taking place in their own bodies. Bulk and heft were developing; they were lengthening, fattening up; the space they occupied was more than what it had once been.

Sashaying in smooth curves they felt glimpses of the future twitching and jolting beneath their tightly bound silver skins.

This was the time when the call of the salt first made itself heard, beating in dull tones beneath the familiar noises of the day. In the settled stillness of night was it most audible, a distant hum hanging at the edge of consciousness.

Weaving between their fellow salmon, sharing with them the river's fare, Freda and Jacob pushed gently at each other, testing the boundaries of what their changing bodies could do.

Either one would begin it, darting at random in some unnamed direction, pulling the other along an unfolding path without word or warning. Sometimes the follower would take a few seconds to pick up the route and the leader would spin and wait, watching and smiling at the confusion sown.

In pinwheels of delight the two young salmon would crash through their world oblivious to all but the moment, amalgams of energy loosed from their moorings, sent careering into the water jubilant and joyous, life seeping from every part of their bodies, splintering the boundary between here and there, you and I, the self and its surroundings.

On and on they would drive, refashioning the dance of their first meeting a hundred times over, coaxing symphonies of movement from the flex and pull and jerk of muscle, tail and fin, drawing newer and newer life from the source of their companionship, reigniting the flames of delight with ever-deepening breaths, the flames growing and growing in intensity, burning hot and white and fierce until the shuddering, all-encompassing moment in which each of them disappeared into one another and all that remained was speed and whip and light coated in the water's silken shroud.

Such being the nature of things, the sun's descent marked the passing of the day. Freda and Jacob, both sated, both full, left the water's body. Together they made their way to the depths, looking for rest and the chance of renewal, ready for morning.

Floating quietly next to each other, among the shadows and vegetation of the river's hard floor, the two salmon spoke of things they could not name, in ways they did not quite comprehend but which, as we have all had cause to realise, were the necessary precursors to a divination of the truth that waits, behind the veil, to be fully disclosed.

'What do you think is out there, beyond the river?' she asked.

Jacob shrugged his fins and looked at Freda.

'There's so much we don't know. Like that time we leapt, when we jumped into the air. How much land is there? What's it made of? I sometimes think about that day and wonder how many other rivers there are. If salmon are everywhere, living like we live.'

Her voice tailed off as speech ran into memories.

Jacob turned away from her.

'I heard some of the older ones talking about something a few days ago,' he said. 'They were saying they'd been further away from here than anyone else. Said they swam until they couldn't see us any longer, until the river became a different world.'

Freda moved her head towards him.

'Two of them went further than the rest. Travelled on by themselves. Ended up alone. I heard them speaking about it. They said they met another salmon – much older. An adult.'

'Did they say what he looked like?'

'Big. Big and tired they said. As if he wasn't much longer for the river.'

Freda shivered.

'They didn't approach him at first, just stayed a little bit away until they knew it was safe. Then they went up to him, slowly, because they didn't want to shock him. They were nervous, they said, both of them. Ready to flash back upriver if he didn't react well.'

'What happened?'

'Well, he was tired this salmon, and when they came round the front of him and saw his face up close, they knew he was in a bad way. There were tears and rips in his scales and his eyes were half-dimmed, like he was trying to sleep and stay awake at the same time.'

A little surge ran through the water, shaking the vegetation. They both kicked their tails and rode it, holding their positions while it passed.

'These two salmon went up to him and asked him if he was alright.'

'What did he say?'

'Nothing, at first. His eyes opened a little and he just looked at them. They said they swam round him, trying to see if he had a bad injury or something but it seemed like he was beaten up all over. When they went back to speak to him something had changed. A light had come over his face and his eyes were wider than before. Brighter too. Almost shining. He wasn't moving much, and his voice was weak – cracked and broken, they said, like it was the leftovers of something once great and powerful.'

Freda pulled herself closer to Jacob. She held her fin against his, followed the line of his sight into the depths.

'They said they didn't ask him any questions, he just started talking. Right there, like that, staring at them, with these huge eyes. Started talking and talking. At first they couldn't tell what he was saying, thought it was gibberish, but then they began to pick things out.'

'"The sea," he kept saying, "the sea." There were other things too, but he kept coming back to that.'

'What else did he say?'

'He looked at them both, I mean really looked at them, as if before he'd only been looking through them, staring at something else that wasn't there – or maybe he couldn't even tell that these two salmon were in front of him. But now he was looking at them, fixing both of them with those eyes of his.'

'And he said: "The sea's waiting for you. It's always there, waiting. There's no beginning and no end to it. No bed or bank. The sea is the sea is the sea. Salt, plenty and death. That's what it is. All of us are made for it. The sea is waiting."'

Jacob's words stalked the path of silence. Neither he nor Freda could bring themselves to speak. The dying salmon's prophecies repeated inside their heads, rolling around, scraping along the sides, rattling. They stayed close to one another, fins touching. Gradually, as the heat of the story faded and the darkness strengthened its pull, they sank into sleep.

*   *   *

It was an inauspicious day. Grey clouds. Thick, dripping towels wrapping the sky. The air sharp and wet.

Past the land, the salt water heaved and sighed. Waves broke the slick hills of the surface, crashed down upon themselves, shattered into streams of white froth.

High above, gulls called, echoing the movements of the swell, riding the circling currents in wing-glide arcs and spirals.

A few miles inland, the shoal was passing along the straightening line of the river. Here the meander had been tamed. Banks bowed to one side and then the other, but the trend was to the centre.

In the flow, chatter among the fish bubbled and spat like oil excited by the heat of the pan. Leith's information was sound; today the sea would meet them, or they, at least, would meet the sea.

In the right-hand side of the pod the five friends swam together, Jacob and Freda at the back, Leith at the front, using his large frame to cut the water. His body punched through the liquid, creating a wide slipstream in which his companions conserved energy and awaited their turns at the front.

'What do you think it will be like?' asked Elu.

'There could be anything out there.'

'Anything at all,' said Jacob. 'Things we've never seen before.'

'Do you think there will be many other salmon?'

'Maybe,' said Lox.

'Yeah, maybe.'

Freda listened as they talked, the pain in her tail returning more often than she had hoped it would. As the conversation wandered through orchard after orchard of exotic hopes and speculations, she felt her own mind drifting away.

Lacking focus her eyes left her kin and took in the passing banks, vegetation, and the brief, blurred outlines of creatures scuttling, swimming and darting away from the shoal.

She could feel herself as part of the school. It was instinct, working below the wit of her conscious mind. She knew she didn't need to attend closely to her movements. A unity hung over them, one earned in the moments of the first break and strengthened in the days that followed.

The dominance of her vision waned as she shrunk back into herself. Jacob's words – those of Lox and Elu – softened and dispersed. She was aware of only faint murmurings, voices bleeding into a burr, single and indistinct.

Here the river ran fast and true. It was wide. It was deep. Freda felt its force around her. She sensed the pull and press of the current. Each of them could ride these flows with ease now.

How their confidence had grown, she thought to herself, in so short a time.

And it was here that her mind turned once more, not to the sea, but to the past.

She thought of the river, of the life they had lived within its borders, of the sustenance it had provided; of the luck and guile that had played their part in bringing every one of them to this point; that had deserted those, so many in number, who had fallen by the wayside, their bodies now subsumed into the life they had left behind.

She thought of the days that had passed among the calm waters of her birth, the days in which she and Jacob had played without restraint, in which they had swum beneath a protective cloak visible only in retrospect.

She thought of her memories, asked herself whether they would remain or whether they would shift and change like the river.

The events that had shaped her rolled across her mind. Each one loomed for a moment, took over the entirety of her senses, and then dissolved into the distance, waning, fading, replaced by the next image in the succession.

How had her life become these singular moments, she wondered, each suffused with feelings and emotions she could barely recall as the vivid colours they had once been? As the electric shapes and sounds that had riven hot lines across her scales?

What would become of her away from the river? How would she retain these fleeting memories of herself amid the space and distance and depth of the sea? Would she still be Freda Salmon when the salt water took her and the river was but a thing once known, brief and transitory, where previously it had been the very essence of all she was and knew – the totality of her world and the reflection and origin of her soul?

Freda felt herself falling away from the shoal. Her body pulled into itself and she shrunk and shrunk until barely any of her remained. Away the other fish swam, growing more distant with each passing moment. The river called to her. Through the current she could hear her name being called in tones thick with familiarity and the comforts of home. The river spoke, beckoned her to return, pulled at her with warm, gentle arms and led her slowly away from the school and the nearing brine.

She was floating through the water, drawn upstream by the heart of the river. Everything she had known, everything she had seen, everything she had lived tore past her as she gained speed. All the days and the seconds and the minutes and the hours of her time in the water were reversed. They shot back through her as she tumbled towards the first moments of her life. They pressed up against her flesh; fell into the spaces that marked the boundary between then and now; fizzed across the diminishing surfaces of her mind; sucked light and shade and shadow from her eyes until nothing remained but the darkness of creation.

She felt herself dissolving into the flow.

The edges of her body began to crumble. Piece after piece left her. As they fell away, each chunk of flesh vanished into the river's tumult, breaking into a thousand pieces, each consumed by the violent thrust of the water, accentuated by the clash with Freda's opposite movements, upwards through the flow.

Ever less of her remained. Jerked through the speeding force of the current it seemed like the water was cleansing her of every ounce of worldly matter. On and on she raced, her own heart beating as one with the heart of the river, her own mind seeping into the ancient mind of the water.

All sense evaporated within the liquid torrent.

No light shone. No shape played. No sound called.

No words broke the blackness.

No body and no bone remained to encase Freda Salmon.

All was the river, and the river was all.

Freda, what endured beyond the confines of eye and bone and fin and scale, pulsed and surged in absolute union with the tumbling flesh of the water; that which persisted, that which survived, coursed along the current in the same way that life had coursed along the veins of the Freda who had lived before the dispersal of time and the triumph of unceasing energy. She breathed fire through the river's body; it breathed fire through her. And together they rasped the flames of life into every single thing they touched, conjuring heartbeats and breath out of desiccated absence, bringing light to the shadows and singing voice into the hollow mouths of soil, leaf and skin.

And then a scream broke her reverie as the tide of life ebbed from one shore so that it might flow upon another.

In the air a dagger, shooting towards the water, fixed upon the transmutation of blood and flesh into survival.

*　　　　　*　　　　　*

Fire through dry grass.

The first scream to pierce the shoal sliced the group in half.

Confused and frightened, fish shot away from the noise, cast themselves hard and fast through the water.

More screams came as other salmon sighted the eagle, the shared inheritance telling all who saw it that this high-slung patch of brown, flashed with yellow and scarred with white, was the Reaper incarnate, coming to lift them from the river and remove them from the course of life itself.

Jets and eddies swirled inside the flow. Bubbles burst behind the tails of incoherent fish moving without design, zigzagging, rising, falling, losing themselves and their senses amid the current.

Freda fell over herself. For a moment she could not tell what direction was up. Spiralling through the water she saw the bank then the sky then the floor racing to meet her.

She tried to right herself. Pain fired in her tail. She moved too late and felt the crunch of her underside against the hard stone of the river's bed.

Salmon flew across her eye-line. Fish she recognised from the pod. Others she didn't.

Lox appeared for a second, struggling against the push of the water. As quickly again he was gone. Freda groped after him with her eyes, scanning the liquid squall rushing across her face.

There was no sign. She felt a sense of panic rising up inside her chest as she realised she could see nothing beyond the few inches immediately in front of her.

Having bounced off the riverbed she had slowed, but only a little. Her body was not yet her own again. It cut and slashed through the water under the force and thrust of the current.

Straining, she tried to regain her poise. Muscles flexed against the river. Her fins stuck out; flat and firm they fought to slow her pace, resisting the hard pull of the flow.

In a moment she was stationary, now angrily beating her fins and tail, trying to maintain her position for a few seconds more. Her head was shaking, her eyes scanning, searching for purchase.

The river roared around her. It screamed and balled and shouted. Ahead she could see two rough groups of salmon, split in the middle by an acre of cold, empty space. She blinked, shook her head, tried to see them more clearly.

Above, the brown sword hung in the air, waiting to drop.

And then the cord was cut.

Falling, the eagle drew in its body, straightened its neck. Two giant fans unfolded. Claws opened up, long sharp talons curving inwards, ready to close themselves around the trunk of an oily body, to pierce the guts and wrench the flesh out of one world and into another.

Desperate, trying to hold her position, Freda watched as the eagle fell, gaining speed. She watched as it broke the surface of the river and plucked a salmon from the furthest group. She stared, frozen, as the fish was taken, as the eagle's wings beat an anarchic rhythm, as it lifted itself back into the air, absenting a life from the world in which it had grown and endured, intent on nothing but its own purpose as it soared higher and higher, wings settling into the smooth repetition of the factory bellows, an infant's cry calling in its ears, decrying its parent in strident tones of congenital hunger from the high safety of the eyrie.

And all Freda could think was 'Jacob.'

She flattened her fins against her side.

The power of the river thrust her forwards, squeezing the breath out of her. Fear surged behind her eyes, sweeping away sense and reason.

She slashed her tail, flicked and whipped her body. She lost sight of the pod from which the eagle had taken its prize. She lost sight of everything as her heart crashed into the walls of her chest and the water around her grew hot and angry, wrapping her up in thin, silvery slivers of dread.

Everything was the liquid, pressing and pushing, shaking her around, tossing her like a rag doll.

She strained.

Her body groaned. Her tail cried.

She strained.

Clarity returned. Her vision cleared. She saw other fish ahead of her. She was not the only one rejoining this half of the group. There were other salmon she did not recognise. They were following similar paths, from the sides, from below; trying to regain the safety of numbers; seeking to reconstruct the alliance shattered by the scream and the eagle.

Here the river was wider again; these waters marked the outer edges of the estuary. The muscular pull of the tide began to make itself felt. Salt seeped across the freshwater boundary, marking its territory and calling to the familial memory of the salmon, calling to the memories that were not their own, those seeds of the past lived first by others and forever waiting to be lived again.

Before Freda could say anything, before she could call out to her fellow fish, before she could let loose a single volley of Jacob's name in the anxious, fearful hope that it would be returned, another eagle made its attack.

She had not had cause or chance to notice this second hangman circling above the river's thickening width.

But now both of those arbiters of existence – cause and chance – weighed heavy upon her.

Barely a foot ahead the eagle broke the surface, tearing a hole through the water's liquid shell.

Every tendon and muscle inside Freda's body howled.

An ageless presence she only half-recognised wrenched her body still.

Right in front of her eyes two bright yellow claws encircled the wriggling flanks of a male fish. Sharp points pierced the skin of his belly. They pressed, tightening as they sensed the certainty of having made the catch.

Freda saw the flesh split. She saw the talons prise holes in the orange and sliver scales so like her own. She saw the first pull of the eagle's legs as it began its ascent, jerking the terrified, squirming fish out of the water, pulling the salmon into the cold, alien worlds of land and air.

As they rose, she caught sight of the salmon's mouth, open and despairing, sucking at the air, drowning amid the plenty that offered everything to so many but which, to this prisoner, offered nothing but the thin, tired hands of death.

In shock, staring up at the heavens, through the reconfigured surface of the river, her body flushed with adrenaline, a temporary shelter hiding the pain and fatigue that swam below, Freda felt herself buffeted from behind.

Another fish knocked against her as he raced passed, scurrying further into the salt.

It jolted her back to the present.

There was no way of knowing how many eagles were circling in the skies above. There was nothing to suggest only two were hunting near the river's mouth.

She shook herself, looked only ahead, fired herself into the fading slipstream of the fish just gone.

Speeding forwards, she dived towards the river's floor. Her body called to her, imploring her to slow down. Her tail sounded a siren of pain.

But she persisted. She would not be cowed. Everything she knew and felt told her to move, not to succumb to the desires against which she fought.

A change in the light, the world above altered.

She sensed the displacement of water. This time she did not look. Her eyes stayed fixed ahead, following a line only inches above the hard surface of the estuary floor. She did not tarry, denied the effects of surprise. Did not reel. Did not falter. She had not come this far, been through this much, to be stopped now. She would not allow it. She willed all that she had against it, whipped it up into a beating, swirling vortex of certainty and belief.

The feeling and reflection and assessment of all this would have to wait. The last veils of youth, blowing gently in the breeze, had finally left her – later than even she had realised, just as the scent of perfume leaves a room in which it has lingered long after the wearer has moved on.

Quickly were her efforts rewarded. Within moments of a third attack, she caught the group she was chasing. She secreted herself in the middle of the shoal, slipping between the thrashing tails of fast-swimming fish she did not recognise.

The water was deeper here. It moved with greater force; the energy of the tide made itself known in strong, heaving pulls. Salt permeated the world. It was the boundary. No longer river. Not yet sea.

How big the school was Freda could not say.

Safe at the centre of its protective cocoon she allowed herself a moment's rest. Looking around she wondered how many of the original group were here.

Half? Two-thirds?

She could not be sure.

Now, as she cast her eyes left and right, trying to penetrate to the edges of the closely-packed shoal, she realised how much her, Jacob and the others had been their own unit travelling within a larger mass – one which was unknown to them except in as much as the familiarities of birth and the species played out across the skin, flesh and bone of all who were a part of it.

And what of Jacob? She would have to wait until they were fully in the sea before she could begin to search for him. Her stomach turned and knotted as she thought of the uncertainty that was to come. Skipping from fish to fish she would have to look into the eyes of all if she were to have any chance of finding him.

It didn't seem right that she should shout his name into the belly of the school, however much she longed to do so. She was alone here. Surrounded by fish she did not know. Anxiety hung heavy, pulled down on her, denied the importance of her desires.

Alone now, in the safety of her unknown kin, she had time to think. Fear wrapped its tendrils around her thoughts. It was the fear she had tried to limit, tried to bury somewhere deep and distant, that she had pushed away and sought to reject.

What if he wasn't here? What if he had split in the opposite direction when the eagles had wrought their carnage, severing the shoal?

And of course, beneath this first layer of fear, beating and breathing like the unspent energy that lurks in the volcanic vents of the ocean floor, there was a deeper layer: the terror of absolute, unequivocal loss that threatened to escape and engulf her if – if – Jacob had been one of those who was taken.

Without respite the group ploughed on. They cut a line across the body of the estuary, driving themselves into full communion with the salt.

Around them the world grew. Deeper, wider. Banks disappeared, melting away into false echoes wrongly perceived through the shifting waters. No riverbed existed here. There were only the unfamiliar furrows and falls of the sea floor.

Something inside the salmon drew them on. All could sense it. All could taste it, sitting lightly on the edges of their tongues. Pulses and intuitions made flesh: the inheritance of their ancient kin making itself known in this strange territory, telling them they had been here before, even if it was in another lifetime, one forever unlived and forgotten.

Tension in the shoal began to dissipate. Fish allowed themselves to drift from the tight formation that had scored its way through the water under threat of attack.

Freda looked around her as she swam. She looked into the great, unfolding depths of the sea. Looked up towards the light, here somehow different from what it had been in the river. Looked down at the rock and sand beneath, watched it slowly falling away.

So much was here. So much still to be explained and explored. So much that would change her.

She knew that now. Understood it in a way that words could not capture.

The safe and settled life she and Jacob had known felt like the memories of another fish. Refracted through the lens of the salt she questioned what truth it had possessed at the time of its being lived, let alone what truth it held for her now, as she felt the magnetic pull of the feeding grounds guiding her further and further from the place of her birth.

What is real if all is change? She asked herself. Who am I if not the things that made me? But where are those things now and how can I believe in them when they have brought me to this point?

She did not bother to make her way through the channels and gullies of the school, those spaces that had opened up as the group had begun to relax.

She did not bother to search in the eyes of all those fish with whom she was travelling.

She did not bother to call Jacob's name.

For she knew he was not there.

And, as the sea took them all into its great bulk, she wondered if she too had been left in the river.

Part Four – Salt

The sea was not the river.

It was a different world.

Where the river flowed the sea heaved. Where the river moved, running across smooth rocks and flattened sand, shaped by years of pressure exerted by the current, the sea lunged and withdrew, held on the edge of a pendulum, forever swaying back and forth under the totalising pull of the tides.

Where the river was fresh the sea was salt. Where the river sparkled with purity in the light of the morning sun the sea subsumed luminescence, filtering out the rays that fell upon it, refusing to allow all but a few beyond the first few metres of its depths.

Where the river was beholden to the influence of the weather, the sea was weather itself. Where the river grew and receded beneath the rainfall and the meltwater that became it from the mountains and the skies, the sea was a conduit for the swathes of energy that marshalled themselves far away from the desiccating influence of the land.

Waves pushed the surface of the salt water high above itself. With hastening force, they departed the burgeoning arc they had begun and crashed back down, slashing momentary holes in the water's dark, rippling skin.

In times of stillness, when the anger and the vitriol of the skies had dissipated, leaving behind no trace of the power that had animated the vast storm clouds and swirling winds, the world above the sea was notable only for the scarcity of life that existed there.

In the expanse, human vessels cut their lines of travel like Bedouin marking slow, encumbered time across the hot, endless sands of the desert. Birds swept and circled in the air, some passing over the water on their way to distant breeding grounds, others moving, diving and settling for brief periods, dragged down by the sight of food swimming beneath the unbroken film of the surface.

But for all the thoughts one might have of the spread of gulls and albatrosses, terns and petrels, these were no more than pinpricks of colour on a canvas of white.

For ultimately, and in stark contrast to the river, which resided within the land, ensconced and intertwined, a giver and sustainer of life to those around it, the trees, plants, creatures who lived their days in the air as well as those who survived and flourished within the water, the sea was concerned with that which became it, with the world it engulfed. Here everything was subsumed beneath the salt-crust of the waves. Some may fend atop this, picking up sustenance from the first few feet of the depths or, in the case of humans and the extensions of themselves they raised from wood, metal and disparate fibres, from somewhere deeper. In the end, however, the sea was the sea was the sea, a world within a world, separate and distinct, excised from the land and the air and the freshwater that passed through each. It spoke in different tones, felt with different senses, lived a different life.

*   *   *

'Did you come from upriver?' asked Freda.

'Yes. All of us did.' The salmon moved its head to indicate the nearest dozen or so fish.

'The sea's a different place, isn't it?'

'Very different.'

No more was said.

The fish kept swimming, eyes ahead, tails moving, passing through the salted water.

*   *   *

It was night. The sky was sheathed. There was no light.

The shoal was resting some way beneath the surface. Here the water was cooler, though the dregs of the sun's rays still reached this point, albeit in reduced form.

Freda was alone.

All around her there were salmon from the river, but she could not put a name to any of them. And had they been called to speak hers, each would have remained silent.

She thought of the river and of Jacob. So too of Leith, Lox and Elu. She wondered where they were, whether they were still alive. Most of all she wondered about Jacob. Wondered with a heart that sagged and swung, burdened by absence, by the sadness and the doubt this brings.

With the passing of time and the gaining of distance her experiences of the eagle attack had dulled. Now she could let her mind take over from her senses and remind herself of how unlikely it was that he had been one of the fish taken by the birds.

Yet all the rationalising in the world cannot fully extinguish the flames of passion once they have been lit; perhaps only time as lived over a deepening span of years can do that; perhaps only death, of one sort or another.

*   *   *

As the sun had risen and fallen, as the waves had reared up and collapsed beneath their own weight, as the tides

84

had heaved and pulled across the unfathomable acres that separate land from land, so the salmon had continued their journey, swimming together in search of the memories bequeathed to them by their ancestors.

Freda left the middle of the shoal and made her way to the front.

Here, the largest fish were taking it in turns to cut a line through the salt. Groups of three worked together, forming themselves into a V-shape that created a profile for the rest of the school to follow.

At first, she struggled to keep up. She slipped backwards into the pack, the force of the water taking her by surprise.

Resetting herself she pushed to the front again, this time more slowly, edging past various fish until she was in the row behind the leading three.

She soon found herself at ease with the pace. Her body was more developed now. It had responded to the challenges of the journey. She could feel the greater strength she possessed. The wound in her tail had healed over. It no longer hurt, even if the mark of injury remained.

Around her, the larger fish became aware of her presence.

Eyes swivelled. Where once they would have pierced the shell of her skin, asking questions and probing the regions of insecurity, now they skated across Freda's scales before returning to the onward stare, satisfied by the confidence and belief with which they had been presented.

The sea was changing Freda. She knew she was alone now. If anything were to come, beyond the bare needs she shared with all else that seeks to survive, it would be at her own behest.

For two days she travelled at the front of the shoal. Silent. Unflinching.

On the third day she spoke.

'The river didn't prepare us for this, did it?'

She asked it to the water, sent it drifting forwards without direction.

A fish to her side responded, as if the question were intended only for him.

'No, it didn't. I never thought it would be like this. So much space and size. It's endless. So far from the river.'

'Sometimes I wonder if the river's even there. I mean, how could we know? How could we ever say whether all of that still exists?'

The fish nodded.

'It crosses my mind, sometimes. Out here you begin to feel like it was a dream.' He flicked a fin and nodded into the empty vastness.

'I remember this day,' she said. 'It feels like years ago now. I was swimming with someone, someone I used to know, and we were throwing ourselves through the water. Just darting and flashing wherever we wanted. No thoughts for anything else. I – we – felt so free back then. Like nothing mattered.'

'And now we're here,' said the fish, 'older and wiser.' He chuckled. 'Or maybe we were wiser back then, before all this.'

'I can still remember it,' said Freda. 'The more I think about it the nearer it seems to get. We could be there now, in the river, swimming with the current.'

'Maybe we are. Maybe this is just a bigger river.'

'Maybe it is,' she said.

And the shoal swam on.

* * *

'Stephen,' said the fish.

'Freda. Nice to meet you.'

They both smiled.

It was the next day. The two of them had dropped to one side of the front of the school. Here they could talk more easily.

'Where do you think we're going?' asked Stephen.

'Somewhere with food, I think. It feels like all this effort must be for a good reason. I reckon by the time we arrive there'll be more food than we could imagine.'

'I hope so. I could see myself enjoying that. More food than the river. There must be, mustn't there? Otherwise, why would we have come?'

Freda shrugged.

Stephen flexed his body and shook his head.

'All that food there, waiting for us. It's going to be glorious!'

Freda smiled.

'It will be good, yes.'

A pause unwound itself between them.

'There must be something else though. Don't you think? Those days when we were in the river, towards the end, when the salt and the sea were calling. Everyone was so nervy. It was like waiting for an explosion. All of that – and this – just for food? I know it's important but I kind of thought there would be more than that.'

'Well, it's a while to go yet, I'm sure. Maybe there will be more when we get there. Who knows?'

'There was more in the river,' said Freda.

Stephen nodded, though he did not speak.

*   *   *

Dusk returned and the salmon rested. The water was calm.

It was a clear night. Black studded with diamonds. A lone ship broke through the cool waters, odd lights here and there casting tokens of illumination into the darkness. On board, the people slept. Only a few lived in the night-time; those charged with maintaining course; those who did not want the light.

'Jacob. He was called Jacob.'

Stephen turned and saw Freda looking at him. They had changed positions; he on the inside and she now on the outer edge of the shoal's flank.

'We were separated in the estuary. When the salt began taking over. There was an attack. Eagles falling out of the sky.'

'I remember,' Stephen murmured.

'Everything was so much of a blur. The pack split in two. I had to make a choice. I went for the larger group, tried to reach them. 'Safety in numbers,' I thought.'

'I'd have made the same choice. Anybody would have. It was the right thing to do.'

'But that's what took us apart, isn't it? I don't even know if Jacob made it to the other group. He might have been carried off by one of the eagles. He could have ended up alone, without anyone to travel with.'

'Do you think that, Freda? Do you think he didn't make it? Do you think he's not out there somewhere, heading for the feeding grounds like the rest of us?'

'I don't know. Sometimes. I try not to. I try to believe, I really do. It used to be so easy to have faith in things. The river and the current; Jacob; the ebb and flow of the days. But what can you hang your faith on out here?'

Stephen followed the arc of her fin as it cast an invisible net into the far corners of the sea.

'Something deep down tells me that he's out there, but what if it's wrong? I could be fooling myself. Maybe I'm spinning a story to stop myself from giving up. How can you trust a thing that's always changing?'

'Change is the way of the world, Freda. Even when we were in the river that was true. You may not think it, may not feel it as the truth in your memories, but it's real. It's all we've ever known.'

'I don't agree with that.'

'How can you not? Think what we were like when we first knew the river and then how we were when we left. We changed, Freda. Every day we changed. Always altering, always growing. Being exposed to new things, to shifting light, seasons that grew and shrunk. And the river. What was the river if not an ever-changing thing? The river couldn't exist if it wasn't forever altering. Not one drop of water in that river remained where it was. Nothing stayed the same from the moment we were born. It was like that before we were there, and it'll be like that in the future.'

Freda felt herself descending into Stephen's words. They were clear and familiar. Each one a memory she had known. All of them fitting together like the drops of water that made the river, transforming into a smooth, strong mass that called to her, beckoning her to give herself over into acceptance, to let go and allow the current to carry her.

It wasn't enough. The temptation to release was strong but it could not consume her. Something persisted, itching at the edge of her mind, struggling to emerge from the mangled impressions and shadows that hinted at a second, unvoiced knowledge.

'I know what you're saying, Stephen. And you're right. I know that. But it's not everything, is it?'

Stephen flexed his fins as the water briefly became turbulent.

'Is it not?' he said.

'No. There's something else. I can't … I can't quite say it, but it's there. I know it's there. Something fixed, something beyond all the change. Beneath it maybe.'

'In the river?'

'I don't know. Yes, it was there, at least I think it was. But it might be here as well.'

'So maybe it never left. Or maybe it wasn't to do with the river in the first place.'

A pause. Neither of them certain. One of them angry without being able to say why.

'Maybe it's you,' he said. 'Maybe it's in you.'

'Or in all of us,' she replied.

*   *   *

Time slipped by and the school progressed through the deep, unbroken leagues of the sea. Freda continued to hold her place near the head of the group. At her instigation conversations began to blossom. Further back her name gained currency; there were not many fish of her size so close to the front.

It came to pass that, on occasion, the shoal would encounter other groups of salmon making the same journey as themselves. These fish had started from different points along the coast or travelled at different speeds. Some had been fractured and split by harsher currents, some by the shocking violence of attack.

So it was that the school grew, subsuming the kin, close and distant, upon which it happened.

The world of the river was cast deeper into the backwaters of Freda's mind, although a small light still shone, a faint echo still sounded, refusing to let her forget the unspoken knowledge she had tried and failed to name.

Stephen continued to swim close to her. The two salmon opened up as the days went by. They talked of the sea, of the future, of the everyday matters that assail us all. Things of irritation, of absurdity, of laughter and of surprise.

There were moments when both felt the pull of that earlier conversation. It tugged at them gently, asking with great delicacy whether it might be allowed to return.

They came close, each one of them, at different times, but the counterbalance of habit and informality, maturing daily, proved too strong an opposition.

＊   ＊   ＊

Despite the enormity of the sea and the ease with which absence falls upon you there, not often is it truly so.

They were not alone.

It started with a feeling deep within the bowels of the shoal.

The fish sensed a change far beneath them. The water started to rise. It pressed. Pressed until they had to mimic its movements.

Salmon after salmon adjusted, responding to the growing closeness of those below.

A few questioned what was happening. Some shrugged and said that was why those ones were at the bottom. Most simply did what was necessary and paid no more attention.

The water became more aggressive, moving like strong wind, gusting through the school's composure.

Brute force now, driving upwards through the mass, shoving every fish out of place, throwing them here and there, away from the group and into the empty expanses of salt water.

Freda heard a scream, then another. She felt herself being pushed forwards, saw those around her flying away, their tails and fins flashing through the brine. She started to spin. The world tipped upside down. Bubbles streamed. More pressure, more force. Everything thrusting upwards. The water moving like it had never moved before, driven by some unknown energy rising through the depths.

She tried to hold her position, spread her fins out, struggled against the momentum.

Still she was spinning.

With each twisting arc she caught sight of other salmon. They were writhing and thrashing in the salt, beating their fins, jamming their tails against the swirling brine.

Briefly, she made eye-contact with another fish. The look of fear and doubt seeping, unrestrained, from the glassy lens fired a shudder along her spine.

Change.

Sudden change.

Change in everything.

Colour, sound, smell.

Shifting pressure.

Grey, heavy, hard.

Vast.

Vast.

Vast.

Water rushing away from the centre, thousands of litres displaced in cascades, fired off in pulses, transformed into whirling streams, beaten forward in violent rushes.

A grey mountain, rising upwards, bricolage skin; shells sewn into a thick, dull hide; water cavorting in the tiny valleys cut between the barnacles.

It rose, rose as if it was the river itself, steaming out of the darkness, making for the thin light beyond the surface of the sea, dragging the endless banks and beds up towards the world of air and cloud.

Still it rose, pressing through the water like light gliding through glass; unfettered, moving with the grace and ease bestowed by size, ploughing a furrow wider than any other living creature could manage, driving itself upwards with long, slow flicks of the tail; its belly a muscular fist pounding out a rhythm, beating the drum that drives the engine that sweeps the ancient limb through the water like hot iron through snow.

Freda could not breathe.

Her mouth was nailed shut, her gills frozen solid.

She watched as the huge bulk of the whale slid past.

A fin, small in comparison to the groaning stretch of the creature's side, giant in comparison to everything that comprised Freda Salmon, swept forwards in a silk-smooth press before whipping down in the direction of the distant sea floor, expelling power from inside the whale, sending it out into the salt water. A burst of energy, uninhibited, transmitted across the brine, in Freda's direction.

She felt herself sailing backwards.

Water surged.

Right and left she saw fish flailing in the mountain's break. An eruption of salmon and whale, of salt and flesh.

The moments passed like weeks, passed like childhood car journeys of indeterminate length; passed like the silence of an empty morning when no clock ticks and no voice speaks.

Force.

Force and power subsuming a world within a world. Illuminating the impermanence of the salmon's lives; breaking apart the shell they had woven, that had held firm since they first breached the outer reaches of the river's border.

Freda was moving faster than she had ever moved in the sea. Faster than she had moved since the days of the river. She felt herself rolling. Rolling without control, moving at another's command, totally beholden.

The flow whipped her round. She spun hard. Memories called from her muscles.

Grey.

Darkness.

Light filtering.

Grey.

Salmon.

Tumult; water; engorged streams; froth and foam, whisked up and violent.

Grey, leaving. Rising.

Control. Fighting for control.

The spin slower. The muscles contracting.

Tail.

Fins.

Body flexing.

Fighting. Still fighting. Harder.

The water a friend again.

She was riding it. Using the force to hurl herself upwards, in search of the light.

She was flying. Flying through the water, tail slashing gaping wounds out of the brine, fins pushing against the salt, driving her up and up and up.

So too the whale. Grey and vast and bedecked in the shells and hairs of the barnacles. Lighter markings on its underside revealed as its body passed on, almost vertical, reaching for the water's limit.

Freda, scratching at the edges of her forbearance. Reaching the boundaries of old and jumping forth, unhindered and reckless, seeing the diminishing lengths of the water, feeling the growing weight of the sun and the light, sensing the past resurgent inside of her, faith's flickering fire greedily sucking in oxygen, burning with a heat for so long forgotten, glowing like metal melting in the forge.

Together they passed on.

Freda and the whale puncturing the edge of the world.

In the air, triumphant, tail flapping, Freda saw a great plume erupt from the whale's blow hole. The creature left the water. As it broke the surface it turned, hung in the air, floating, revelling, thick and wide and vast, transposed to another world for a short moment.

Freda started to descend. She saw the sea beneath her, felt the tepid rays of the sun upon her back. In the corner of her eye she could make out the whale, its outline and its shape, the thousand hues of grey rainbowed across its surface.

It fell from the height of its leap, collapsing horizontally into the water, displacing a deep valley's worth of brine.

As Freda departed the world of air, she glimpsed the terrific sight of the whale bombing its way back into the depths. Spray shot into the air, sparking off in all directions. Volleys of gushing water burst upwards. It was an explosion of life amid the barren expanse of the waves.

Swimming again, back within the water's hold, she struggled to control her speed.

Her intentions changed abruptly, and she felt the torque of braking strain the muscles that ran beneath her glistening, freshly gleaming skin.

The whale's intentions were also altered.

It was returning to the place from whence it had come.

In a sharp diagonal it moved towards her, at ease, slipping through the salt; peaceful; sated.

Freda watched as it neared. She could go no slower. It would take more space to decelerate fully.

The whale would hit her, or it wouldn't. Nothing else could be the case.

All the way she watched it. Saw the grey hulk moving as she moved. Saw also how it was different, removed from the experience she knew. Her mind was at rest. There was no fear here now. She might be crashed towards the depths or sent into the prelude of expiry by a crack of its tail. The knowledge flashed across her mind and raised not a heartbeat. She simply watched as the whale moved and as she moved. A point beyond them both the final arbiter of what would be.

As it passed, their eyes fell upon each other.

Freda stared into the deep, implacable sphere, cushioned by bulging skin cut with dark, shadowed folds. She watched the eye as it watched her. Followed it as it slipped across the space in front. Felt it as it looked at her. Wondered, briefly, what the whale saw. Whether it saw her at all. Whether it saw any sentience, any life, mirrored in the thin, small glass of her own eye.

On it dived. The sphere passed into the edge of her vision then departed, replaced by flank, fin, tail.

Freda hit the point where the whale had been in the seconds after it had left.

The water was agitated, still recalibrating itself in the creature's wake.

She looked down, traced the whale's path as it sunk.

Everything was silent.

There was no sound, no sense, no smell.

Everything was the whale.

And then it was gone. Tail flicking a final time and the world it had entered becalmed once more.

*   *   *

'Come on! Come on! Meet me here. Pass the message back. Send it out as far as it needs to go.'

Salmon were flocking to Freda. The shoal was beginning to re-form. Busy voices were meeting beside her, naming the whale and the power that had split the pack.

'Stephen.'

'Yes,' he said, removing himself from a conversation with a group of fish.

'Circle round the shoal, try and pack them in a bit. Take someone with you if you need.'

Without a word he set off, following Freda's instructions. Two large salmon joined him as he left the edge of the school, their movements sparked by a sound and a jerk of the head.

Freda looked around. She tried to get a sense of how many salmon were yet to return.

One of the largest of the group shuffled through the mass and rose to meet her. She knew him as Sockeye; he had spent the longest time of anyone at the tip of the phalanx. On his tail were two smaller, female fish, one called Muna, who Freda had spoken to before, the second familiar by sight but not by name.

'What does it look like?' asked Sockeye, recognising the steel packed beneath the silver and orange of Freda's scales.

'It's hard to say. I think we're still missing a few but I can't be certain. It feels like some are still out there. I've sent Stephen around the perimeter. He's taken two fish with him. They're going to tighten the group.'

The three salmon nodded their heads.

'They should be able to see if anyone else is nearby.'

'What can we do?' they asked, the words voiced by Muna, but spoken for them all.

'Sockeye, go and find as many of the big fish as you can. Take them to the front and get them to form up. Once you've set the head off the rest will fall in behind.'

'I'm on it,' he said and dipped down into the bowels of the pack.

'Muna …'

'Flo,' said the third fish.

'Right. Flo. Good to know your name. I'm Freda. You two should go through the shoal and spread the word. Tell them this is a warning. We need to swim hard and we need to stay alert. We've come too far to let ourselves get broken up. Tell them we're going to wait a little longer and then we're going to move. It'll put us in a bad position if we stay.'

'OK.'

'And what if they ask who this is coming from?'

Freda looked at them with surprise. It wasn't a question that had crossed her mind.

'I don't know,' she said. 'Tell them Freda. Tell them Freda says we need to move, and we need to remember what we're here for, where we're going. Tell them the whale said so.'

∗   ∗   ∗

Thoughts of the whale had changed from fiery, incomplete impressions to glossy stories smartly packaged and embellished.

The group were moving with a smoothness and a unity greater than what had previously come.

The machinery of the shoal was oiled, light and strong. It etched its mark upon the seawater, parting the brine with sleek efficiency.

Freda had become the unacknowledged leader of the group. She talked the fish up, talked them down, held the fears and hopes of the pod in her fins, dampening the creeping anxieties, fanning the flames beneath their fragile expectations, damaged as they were by time, distance and the slow-numbing repetition of their work and the water in which they had to do it.

She grew close to Stephen.

They spoke once again of deeper things. He offered her space in which to release the tension and the energy that animated her in the leadership of the shoal.

They rested together.

They swam together.

They knew though, even if they did not say, that there was always to be a bridge between them that would not be crossed.

That bridge was Jacob.

And in those times when Freda found herself reviving the fish with whom they swam, she understood that she was also rousing the faith that abided within her own body; the faith that had ebbed and flowed like the tides of the sea but which had never left her, never altered, never shifted or changed other than in its reach; the faith that, at its core, lived on, that reminded her, like a pinprick of light reminds the darkness of daybreak, that hope was a hard flame to extinguish; a light, perhaps, that would never go out.

Part Five – Return

The sea knows no word of man or woman, knows neither the heartbeats of expectation nor the dulled voices of despair. The sea looks without eyes. Lives without life. Moves and turns and heaves devoid of purpose; churns itself in league with the hard, strong pull of the Moon's yoke; whispers in false voices, the stretching tremors of mass and movement mistaken for expressions of mind, lived and living.

At night, when the rough-smooth surface of the brine is deprived of the sun's light, the temporary illusion of heat and hope that plays across its skin in shimmering, reflected energy ceded by the day's absence. At night, when the depths sink into darkness, when the creatures that dwell beneath are bound together in shared privation, when the salt resembles a soft-breathing pit of tar, opaque and unknown, then the reach of life, that blossom-bright crackle that animates the edges and the centres of all that is, feels faint and gaunt, like a thin thread slowly straining to the point of surrender.

At night, when the sea darkens, when it thickens underneath the weight of shadow. When shape becomes silhouette and form fades into uncertainty. When the night and the dark and the water and the sky are one bleak mass. It is then that the world of salt feels as though it is wholly absented from the world we know. Feels like a netherworld, alive and dead in equal measure. Waiting and arriving, falling and rising, growing and decaying.

At night, when the world has turned, removing all light and optimism, if only for those few hours of absence, the brine throws up the mirror we seek to shroud.

How many times did Freda find herself drawn to that mirror, like water to the sea?

She looked deep into the emptiness. Wondered where that emptiness was. Whether it fell outside, within the water's depths, or inside, along the contours of the self she had struggled to know. The changing, shifting surfaces that played out from the centre. Those surfaces that grew and multiplied, collapsed and retrenched like empires of old.

At night, on the occasions when the shoal was moving slowly, when it was resting, when Freda relinquished temporarily the duties of her leadership, then she would look, glass-eyed and silent, into the mirror.

How small the flame could seem in those moments of darkness. How small the nub of certainty could feel, the kernel that bound the shifting landscapes of her soul. How distant the nourishing waters of hope, in which life persisted and survived. Her life. Jacob's life. Stephen's life. The lives of all those salmon who they led; her and Stephen the leaders incarnate; Jacob the shadow at her side that did not lead, not in the way they led, but swam adjacent, equal and unchanging, forever asking the question that lacked a voice to speak it.

The question asked of us all.

To which we must each provide our answer.

And that we answer every day, every moment, every breath.

The question Freda answered every time she fell upon the mirror of the night. The question of hope, of conviction. Of doubt and belief. Of what it is to live beyond the brilliant, dazzling flushes of youth. The question of life and of death. The question of faith.

And though she doubted, in her doubt she recognised the certainty that ebbed and flowed but always, always remained. Not in God, for what is God to a fish? But in two things that bound her to all the world – sea and river, salt water and fresh.

In herself.

In others.

*   *   *

Weeks passed.

The water grew colder as they travelled further north.

Half-hearted murmurs of dissent echocd through the shoal. Upswells of concern bubbling from the tender sores of wounded expectations.

Freda held the group firm. By her words. By her actions.

She was an example, driving forever onwards. Never allowing the creeping thoughts of disbelief to rise too high. Always extolling the virtues of the group and remembering to anyone who needed to listen how powerfully they had felt the pull of the salt in the long-passed days of their youth.

To those who wavered, who named their doubts and made them flesh in their actions, she offered a calming fin and an open ear. And as they spoke, she named to them the inheritance of the species. The shared drive they all possessed. Which beat, quiet and firm, in their scales, showing them the way when no way could be seen. Guiding them through the alien waters of the sea.

And Freda was rewarded, just as Stephen was rewarded, just as all the salmon of the shoal were rewarded, and just, so Freda hoped, as Jacob would be rewarded too, by the first sight of the ancestral feeding grounds.

They came upon them early one afternoon as light rain fell upon the surface of the water and cool, strong currents ran beneath them. Currents that pressed on beyond the plenty that awaited the tired and hungry salmon, currents that followed their own journey of necessity, driven by forces quite different from those that propelled the school.

*   *   *

'Is this it?'

Freda's voice was tentative. Her words quietened by what she could see.

She and Stephen were at the front, among the strongest group of fish.

Stephen did not answer.

They swam on. In the shifting waters, distance was hard to assess.

'If this is it, we'll have made it.'

'There are a lot of fish up there.'

'We might have caught up with another group.'

Freda's stomach buckled and then relaxed. She hushed herself, forbade the thoughts she was thinking to make themselves fully known.

'Maybe they've come from a different river,' she said.

'Uh-huh. Could be. Could be that. Yeah. Or we could have caught some other group up. Either way, that's probably all it is. Nothing major. Just a bit of a surprise.'

'We'll ask them when we get there. Find out which it is.'

'Yeah, sure. Simple explanation I'd have thought.'

'No point passing the word back, they'll see them soon enough. When we know where they're from we'll pass it around.'

As they spoke, they gained on the group.

And all the time, Freda and Stephen believed less and less in what they were saying.

As they came close, they could see that this was not another shoal of salmon. It was not a different pod, issued from a different river. It was not a school caught by the faster pace of Freda's leadership.

No.

It was an edge. The edge of a new world. The edge of a dim memory, one passed on by the bloodline of the species, being reborn as flesh and bone and scale.

Here was an announcement. The bell that first begins the chimes. The word that births the sentence. The sound that names the world.

Before them, growing more distinct, was the edge of their feeding grounds. An edge that ran and ran and ran, slicing through the clear water in an immeasurable tessellation of gleaming salmon, bound by their brotherhood, their sisterhood, their needs, desires and the molten instincts that had carried them thousands of miles through the salt-cracked shell of the sea.

Hundreds of thousands of fish filled the water, swimming and moving in every direction.

The partial light that penetrated the saltwater's surface glinted against silver, orange, brown. Scales shimmered, glossy and slick, momentarily illuminated. Refracted rays bounced from the rich, oiled surfaces of the sea-suckled fish.

Neither Freda nor Stephen spoke.

Words need not be shed in those moments when two travellers stumble together upon the same wonderment.

They slowed, open-mouthed, felt the rest of the shoal moving past them – salmon with whom they had come so far passing one after the other, yelping, delighting, singing as they laid their own eyes upon the treasure for which they had been searching – sensed the electricity of the group crackling across their flanks, watched as the school gleefully diffused itself into the teeming mass of fellow fish, sighed as the weights of duty dropped one by one from their tired skins.

Some stopped as they passed and exchanged a few words. Flo, Muna, Sockeye – all of them circled round and returned. One by one they made their arrangements; spoke of meeting again to revel in the glory of their shared success.

Eventually, the two friends found themselves alone, staring into the shifting mass of their kin.

Still neither would speak; whether it was because the words would not come or because none needed to be said, they could not be sure. But they waited, the two of them, waited as one, watching their prize, letting the senses they had worked so hard to tame open up once more. Bathing in the relief that comes when the peak is crested and the goal is in sight.

For a few, brief moments, Freda felt the pinwheels of her youth returning. Her muscles bled with energy and joy. Her eyes swam and her fins bristled with an intensity long diminished. Every part of her glowed hot and she was reminded that she was alive in a way she had not experienced since that first great leap she and Jacob had taken beyond the river's border. A way that was the very opposite of the panic-swelled sense of life she had known in the face of the eagle attacks, in the face of absence and loss. A sense just as acute, but dark and painful in its form.

Savouring what they had done, the separate journeys they had led – the journey they had shared – Freda and Stephen felt closer than they had ever been. The bridge that remained between them was briefly climbed. Atop, they met each other, saw each other anew, held, for fleeting moments, a look pregnant with all the possibilities that life has to offer. So close they came, in that time, to a new journey, a path not yet cut, visible to them both only in a brief, fleeting moment amid the moving currents of the sea.

Alone, together, on the edge of the beating, breathing throng of salmon, they waited, silent and still.

Yet …

Yet …

So many things called to them. So much indecision swirled about their bodies, their minds.

For so long they had placed their fires and their flames inside cases of stone, wrapped up the erratic, flailing arms of desire, soothed and tempered them, bound them gently and turned their backs, forever repeating the mantra of delay, of waiting, of sublimation of ends so that what truly called to them – not in short-lived switches, flits and darts, but in long, low tones of necessity – could be sated.

But both knew, beneath it all, that they could go no further.

Atop the bridge they stood, so close, so far.

And they waited, not because the path was becoming clearer, making itself known beyond the first partial impressions they could both discern, but because they knew this was the end, not the beginning, and that their journey was over; where the road had been one, so it would come to divide again.

Two different paths were calling.

What had been had been, and no more would it be so.

That was why they waited, why they held themselves, quiet and unmoving.

When finally the time came, it was Stephen who spoke first.

'So, I'll be seeing you, then?'

'You will.'

A moment. So many seconds in which the pendulum held fast, waiting, hanging, at the far reach of its swing; stored energy temporarily delayed.

'And I'll be seeing you.'

'Good luck, Freda Salmon. You see that you find him.'

'Make the most of it,' she said, nodding toward the feeding grounds, 'we've earned it.'

'We have.'

She looked on as he moved off, saw him stutter. Watched as he turned, swam back towards her, made the distance between them less than it had ever been. Felt his smile. Felt his lips touch hers. Heard the whisper, heard the happiness inside it, so too the sadness.

'We made it.'

Then he was gone, subsumed by the shoal and out of sight.

For a few moments more Freda waited and then she too was gone.

A new path beckoned.

*   *   *

The clock ticked.

Two years went past.

Cities grew, towns shrank. Seasons came, dimmed and died; returned once more, exultant and transitory, riding on the swell and wane of the sun's heat. New life issued forth; blossom hung on branches, shed onto the greening floor; leaves, flowers, fruit filled the spaces left behind. Hatchlings made their way into the world, clawing through the eggshell and into the light; furless babes, blind and loud, wreathed in blood and fluid, felt their mothers' touch fastening them to the land. Old life succumbed to the motion of the days; bodies weakened; minds ailed; stalks and stems and trunks fractured, burned and froze; glass, once so smooth, so tough, cracked beneath the pressure of endless minutes passing on; some could bear little more than a few taps from the sharpened fingers of the hours; others finally relented, admitting defeat after years of disregard for the long-foretold inevitability of what lies ahead.

The world turned and so too did the lives of those whose world it was.

The feeding grounds were a place of partial fixity. While the salmon within them moved and grew, changed and shifted as their bodies responded to the plenty on which they feasted, even while the waters were invaded by wave after wave of unknowing species, ignorant and unprepared for the fate that awaited them, the grounds themselves barely altered.

They were insulated from the wider changes of nature. The seasons, what there was of them here, did not register, save for small shifts in temperature. Light and dark's endless push and pull had little impact on the lives of the fish who settled among the rich and fertile waters.

Few predators broke the cycle of the days. The shoal was so big as to be its own deterrent.

Like a greenhouse, this was an environment sufficiently safe and controlled to allow for growth and cultivation far in excess of what might be achieved elsewhere.

In not much time the fish became stronger, bigger. Some fell by the wayside. Some lost themselves in distant backwaters of the sea, pulled away by the same kind of unhooked logic that can seep into even the hardest minds should the conditions for its birth be propitious.

But, by and large, the swarm of orange, brown and silver expanded. Its numbers holding up while its size grew.

Each member gaining. Increasing in bulk and length and girth.

How Freda had feasted in those first days! She often recalled it during the two years she spent among the grounds.

Every salmon had experienced the same. And so conversation could always be made in reference to the ecstasy – the delight – borne by the coming of abundance in the days that marked the segue from hardship to ease.

Singular as she was among so many of her kin, it came as no surprise to Freda that she did not meet a face she knew from the river or the journey through the sea. She was like the young man or woman who moves to the city of millions and soon senses the incredible distances that can develop when so many live side by side, so close to one another.

Despite the absence of familiar faces, Freda did not find herself alone. She made acquaintances, shared meals, words, laughter, pleasure, days and nights with members of the giant shoal. Together they grew, hunted, swam and slept. Together they contributed to the whole, swimming and diving, falling and rising in unison.

Norms were recast amid time's easy flow. The machine hummed. The larder was managed; emptied, refilled, emptied, refilled.

Cosseted by the comforting grip of prosperity, thoughts of faith and doubt settled down inside Freda's mind. Silt travelling to the riverbed once the surge has passed on.

She did not forget Jacob. Could not. Always he was there. Though where once his presence had been like that of a ghost, calling to her from a place that seemed so near and yet so far, now he was a companion, travelling by her side through everything she did.

For, in her heart, beneath the layers of familiarity and stability that built up, coat after coat gently applied as the days repeated themselves in arcs of sustenance and progress, she knew that he lived. That he was sharing the saltwater with her, whether that meant he was here, secreted among the mass, or in some other feeding grounds, far off and away.

How easy faith can be when wrapped in the warm glow of contentment, she thought to herself on more than one occasion (though these thoughts were never voiced. For all the camaraderie there was, for all the acquaintances she made, there was nothing to match the life she and Jacob had known nor, for that matter, the one she had lived in the heaving depths of the salt-soaked sea). How easy it can be to believe with absolute certainty when the rudiments of life are so well provided.

And then, at other times, she questioned this view. Asked herself whether it was indeed true. Or whether the faith she felt in Jacob being with her, even while apart, of his having maintained himself, his life and his existence in the face of the same trials she had endured – perhaps in the face of worse – was a function of the doubt she had experienced.

The searing, painful doubt that had threatened to puncture the edges of the world in which she lived, that had forced her to hold up against the light everything she thought to be true.

No resolution came.

She did not seek one either, not with any real purpose. The faith she held was enough. Enough to sustain her in the grounds and, she knew, or at least believed, enough to keep her in the weeks – the months – that would follow.

In the days when she and her fellow fish would cross the sea once more, marking the return that waited for them all. Just as it had waited for their forebears and for every member of the chain of life that ran from time immemorial to the world as they now found it.

That ran from the shrouded mists of origin to the hard, supple body of Freda Salmon, orange, brown and silver. Strong, powerful and grown. The embodiment of the species. Reimagined forever and again in the endless cycle of greetings and goodbyes, of ascent and collapse, of dawn and death; of all that is and all that was, each of and inside one another, wound together like threads of a rope; stronger, truer, greater for their being bound as one.

*   *   *

Where the first calls of the salt had been dull murmurs issued from an unknown endpoint – smoke smelt on the breeze – the call of the river was met with the hard-lived experience of things already known.

Long before the days of return fell upon the shoal, the days in which many, but not all, would leave the affluence they had made their own, salmon began to speak to each other of what awaited.

'This time, we'll need to prepare. The crossing won't be the same as life here.'

'How will we decide when the time is right?'

'From what I've heard, the current will be with us most of the way.'

'Eat well. It won't be like this out there.'

'Our days here are numbered. Keep preparing for what lies ahead.'

*   *   *

Freda joined the conversation.

She spoke with authority; called on her experiences of leading the school in the days after the whale had surged, crashing through the bonds of the travelling salmon.

She talked of necessity and choice; shared with those around her the importance of restraint, of marshalling the forces of the collective against the unforgiving silence of the sea.

The fish who heard her recognised the truth that ran beneath her words. Her voice was a siren call. It galvanised, emboldened. It named the future and insisted that it would be beholden to them, not the other way around.

Gradually, as the time of return neared, Freda rose like hot vapour, passing through the mass of preparing salmon until she found herself at the top, in the realms of leadership, among the few who knew that they must do the job that the many requested of them. That they demanded of somebody unspecified yet asked in hope and expectation of those specific.

Sometimes, leadership is simply a matter of going first. The risks that others perceive fade to naught when it is seen that steps, calmly taken, do not crumble the ground upon which they fall.

Or, to cast these thoughts in the minds of the salmon: when the path is cut through the brine, and in being so declared, rises like Lazarus, living where once it was dead, so will all those who dared to hope that it might be so join and follow, sensing that exodus is but a fin-beat made behind the first poised slash of another, who is the same in everything except their place in the line.

*   *   *

And so it was that after two years of plenty, Freda Salmon, alongside many thousands of her kin, began the journey that would return them all to the rivers from which they had come.

Some stayed; the feeding grounds never emptied completely. Salmon arrived at different times, grew at different rates, lived in different ways.

It was a large contingent who left. A mass of thick and glossy fish. Each packed full of the energy and power that would see them through the journey.

Freda took her place near the head, swimming unquestioned beside fish half her size again.

'This is it, then.'

'It is.'

'Feels like only yesterday we first arrived here.'

'Funny, isn't it, how quickly time passes?'

'I don't think we'll be thinking that when we're in the middle of nowhere wondering how long it'll be till the river.'

'Well, you were always a miserable one anyway.'

'Just looking out for you lot, that's all. Keeping your fins in the water.'

'My fins are well and truly in the water, don't you worry.'

'I'll second that.'

'Yeah, me as well. There isn't anybody here who thinks this is going to be easy. We're prepared this time. Lessons learned.'

'Well, you just keep hold of those thoughts for when we're out among it, then we'll see who's prepared.'

'Yes, we will. And we'll all thank you for your hard work when we get there!'

A ripple of laughter passed through the group.

Freda left the others to their conversations and swum upwards, tacking diagonally so as to remain parallel with the head of the shoal.

Looking back, she watched as the two bodies of salmon separated.

Fish streamed forwards, peeling away from the group who remained, continuing to occupy the ancestral grounds. Both schools were large, filled with salmon of varying sizes intent on meeting the goals the inherited memory of the species had bestowed upon them.

Freda was a sentry in these few moments. Stationed above the fray, witness to the movements of so many, each possessed of life and mind and body, each a culmination of all that had gone before, similar yet different in the same instance, she saw her own life in fleeting impressions, each vivid and partial; each eroded, passing from fullness, total and complete, to tiny specks no different from those attached to the multitude of fish who swarmed and swam beneath her.

Where once there had been an old, familiar question, known to us all in the days when youth gives way to the duties and obligations, the repetitions and ambiguities of adulthood, here a different question made itself known, laying soft hands upon Freda's flanks, whispering in quiet tones.

What is this if we are no more exceptional than a pebble scattered on a beach? A grain of sand making up but a tiny portion of the shore, sharing everything with uncountable others, all of a type, all the same, but for a smattering of differences?

It was the same question that comes across the eagle when it floats upon the breeze, espying nothing but empty lands passing on for mile after mile.

It was the same question that stalks the minds of men and women when the hands of comfort withdraw, when the groundswell of loneliness rises up and threatens to engulf.

It was the same question that speaks in the dead of night, when all is still, save for the breaths that come and go, counting the seconds, minutes, hours until the day returns and casts aside the growing pall.

It was the question to which Freda would give her answer in the days and the weeks that lay ahead.

*   *   *

The shoal made great progress. Tightly bound, swimming in harmony, they passed through the water in quick, sharp lines.

Time and sustenance had made them into fish far beyond those who had last crossed the sea's depths. Fins slapped like powerful oars. Whip-cracks of force convulsed sleek scales, shimmying the fishes' torsos in ripples of driving energy. Tails slashed from side to side, pushing strong, muscular bodies forwards through the salt.

Freda took her turn at the very tip of the school's form. Each salmon in the leading group knew it was their duty to share the work. One after the other would take the strain, exerting themselves for the good of the shoal before sinking backwards to be subsumed within the mass, such that they might soon recover and be able to give of themselves once more.

For many days this system did its job, hauling the pulsing throng of fish along the path – now familiar where once it had been unknown, secure where once it had been unstable – that showed the way home.

The journey, for once, was uneventful. Here was a group, sizeable and strong, sure in itself and its aim. Familiar with the landscape through which it moved. No longer cowed by uncertainty.

Predators, what few there were, left the school when they alighted upon it, preferring instead to seek easier food elsewhere. Food that was not so well protected. Which did not sit within an army of friends, all joined in the shared determination to complete the mission they had been set.

* * *

After the passage of many hundreds of miles, the school began to disintegrate.

Different rivers called to different fish.

They each heard the drumbeats inside their minds, felt the magnetic pull tug along the lines of their bodies.

Without notice, groups of salmon would shoot out of the shoal.

Sometimes, it was as if the breakaway had been travelling together throughout. At other times, silver, brown, orange shapes appeared from all over the edge of the mass, popping out like buds coming into bloom.

In these cases, the fish would stop, momentarily, and look around. On seeing their kin joining them from out of the school they would start to breathe again, before passing on in search of the water that had birthed them.

The shoal was still fairly big by the time Freda's turn came. Still large enough to afford anonymity, even to warrant significant distance between the head and the tip.

With a nod and a few words to those with whom she had shared the claims of duty, she was gone, bursting from the side of the group, drawn in the direction she knew would lead her back.

In the few moments before she looked, during the time of her solitude, when she was single and alone, ejected from the comfort and safety of the school, not yet formed up with her kin, staring straight ahead into the continuing depths, but so too beyond, through the brine and the tide, past the boundary where freshwater mixed with salt, along the banks and the bed of the river, up towards the mountains and the shallower waters of home, in those moments, as she held herself, steeled herself, hot fire burned inside her chest, raced through her veins, threatened to force itself out of her body, cracking apart the very scales that made up her skin, for she knew, knew with an intensity she had held in check for half a lifetime, that when she turned, when she broke the reverie and afforded herself the glance that awaited, in those few seconds he would be affirmed or denied, taken from her once again or restored, triumphant and whole. And she had no power. Nothing, other than the chance to look.

So, she took what little was before her and turned.

Part Six – Home

He was not there.

As she hung in the water, feeling the swell of the shoal passing behind her, jostling her up and down in the light-rinsed salt, she knew that he could never have been.

Not that he was gone completely, just that she had been foolish to let herself get caught up in the unlikely advent of possibility and chance coming together in front of her.

He would be elsewhere. In another feeding ground, perhaps. In another sea, even. Maybe he had returned to the river already. Maybe he was not yet to return, choosing instead to remain in the brine for longer than her and their kin.

Freda swam on.

She felt the fire wane, stared ahead as it fell away, until only a flickering trace remained.

Heard the blood quieten in her chest.

Tasted the salt and, within it, the first specks of freshwater; a taste she had not known for a long time.

The new, smaller group, the river shoal, came together.

Large, shiny fish mingled and chatted. Familiarity suffused the water, even where there were fish who had not known each other before.

They were bound by the call of the river. Their river.

In each other's eyes they could see a shared history. And so too could they foretell a shared future.

Knowing the drum-calls that beat inside, they could bear witness to the feelings of one another. These did not need to be voiced. It was enough that they were there, binding the separate salmon in unison. Giving them a unity and a purpose they had craved since the days in which they had first set fin and tail upon the saltwater's currents.

*   *   *

'Well, I never!'

A voice met Freda from the side.

'It can't be, can it?'

The voice moved nearer, gained a body; a body that levered itself through the crowd of fish until it was next to Freda, grinning and looking pleased with itself.

'It's Leith. Leith, you remember, from the river. You're Freda, aren't you? Of course you are! I wouldn't forget a face. Especially not one from the river. How've you been? Where've you been, more to the point? I didn't think I'd ever see you again, not in a million years.'

Before she could answer, Leith had swum off, his big, wide body pushing its way through the pack. The hole he cut quickly sealed up behind him.

Freda kept swimming. She looked into the shoal, staring at the place where Leith had been, her eyes bright, mouth open.

She watched on, turning her head now and then to check the way in front was clear.

Nothing happened.

She waited a little longer, continued to watch and check.

Nothing happened.

She began to wonder whether it really had been Leith, or rather some silvered apparition projected from her memories.

'Through here. Mind out, will you? Honestly.'

It was the same voice, moving towards her, pealing out through the school.

She saw the hole open up again.

Through it moved first Leith and then, a short distance behind, Elu.

Freda smiled.

'See, I told you this was the place. How about that, then? Can you believe it? Freda Salmon from the river. Right here. After all that time.'

'Freda! It is you. It really is. We didn't think we'd ever see you again.'

The two fish came up next to Freda and fell into formation beside her. All three of them swam in harmony with the shoal.

'It's good to see you both.'

'I still can't believe it.'

'Neither can I!'

'It's like a gift from the river. It's brought us back together. How about it? The three of us here at the same time. Fantastic.'

'I never knew what happened to you,' said Freda. 'After the attack … it all seems so long ago now … another world.'

'Is Jacob with you?'

'Where is he? Is he swimming further back?'

Freda looked at them both.

She saw her own expectancy in their faces. Saw the hope and anticipation.

' … '

'Don't hold your tongue, Freda. You're keeping us in suspense! Is he at the front then? Doing a bit of leading? Taking us back to the river all on his own?'

Leith and Elu both laughed.

'I don't know,' said Freda.

'Well, he must be somewhere. Front, middle or back. Didn't he tell you where he was going when he left? Doesn't sound like him.'

'No … I mean I don't know where he is. I haven't seen him since … since … I thought, when I saw you … I thought he might be with you. That you might know where he is.'

The light drained from Leith's face. So too from Elu's.

'Oh, Freda. We didn't know. We're so sorry. We always thought he must have gone with you when we were attacked. We didn't know.'

Elu looked away, composed herself.

'Sorry, Freda,' said Leith. 'He was a great fish. One of the best.'

They swam on.

Silent.

Sad.

As the intensity of the salt began to wane, diluted by the growing spectre of freshwater, Elu spoke.

'We lost Lox along the way. I know how it feels.'

'I'm so sorry,' said Freda. 'That's awful. I wish he could be here with us now.'

'Me too. I still think of him, every day. It's hard to shake the memory of someone you love.'

Freda nodded.

'It happened while we were searching for the feeding grounds. A shark found us. Cut the shoal in half. We just kept swimming, those of us who could. Never looked back.'

She paused, shook her head.

'The sea's not the river, that's all I know. Not the river at all.'

Freda thought about this as they carried on. She drew closer to Elu, as if to show her sorrow for Lox's loss; for the fear that must have settled upon them, all of them, when faced with such terror.

'I still believe he's alive,' she whispered.

Elu did not speak. She swam on, her head a little lower than before.

'I have to,' said Freda.

Finally, Elu replied:

'I know.'

*　　　　　*　　　　　*

As the group neared the estuary in which they had first come to know the saltwater they felt the power of the tide pushing them forwards. In heaving rolls of liquid thunder it lurched towards the land, lending the fish speed and movement.

Freshwater and brine mixed, the first continually subsumed by the diffusing force of the second. However much the river might try to rename the salt, it would always fail, caught beneath the power and the expanse of the sea's thrust.

The salmon could taste the changes in their mouths, could feel it in their skin.

And somewhere deeper they felt the change more profoundly. With greater certainty than they had known.

New voices spoke to them, calling in muffled tones from a far-off place. They spoke of return, of home, of purpose and completion.

Although the journey back had been quicker than the one that first took them away from the river, it had still exacted a physical toll on the fish.

Food was scarce. The demands of the sea were high.

While the shoal retained a size far in excess of what it had been some years previously, this did not disguise the fact that each salmon possessed only a finite stock of energy, and that this would have to take them much further than the river's mouth.

Hunger rumbled.

The school strung out as weaker fish began to flag.

Still the tide did its work, supporting the salmon, pushing them forwards faster than they could manage alone.

It rocked and swayed behind them, above them, around them. Wrapped them up in its hands, held them close as it juddered toward the land. Finally, the travellers felt, they were not alone on this journey of theirs. The one that had its origins in those first fitful days of light in the far reaches of the river, that had seen each one descend the flow, cross the deep and make their return, supported by themselves and each other, by the inheritance of the genus. But by no more than that.

Finally, Freda thought, and Leith and Elu too, there was some grain that did not go against them. Some surface that did not rub.

Despite these facts, the salmon continued to propel themselves toward the freshwater with as much power as they could muster. They were too close and too old to risk ceding momentum. The tide was a welcome boon. It was not a surrogate for their own efforts. Merely a supplement.

*   *   *

Nature, unminded and devoid of purpose, extracts no tolls. Where bodies fall and minds tire – that is but the rules by which the game is played, the backswing of the pendulum.

So we cannot say that there was any guiding hand that balanced the press of the tide against the bank of sea lions who waited, as their own ancestors had waited, slick-skinned, whiskered and alert, eyes pricked and poised, for the returning salmon. Waiting for the catch.

The lions pushed off from the beach, their bodies built for the water. Streamlined, they pierced the salt-fresh tide. At first they were ungainly, half-encumbered by the lack of depth. Soon they passed on. Found themselves in deeper water. Began to dive and slice through the liquid, reborn as mammalian fish, returned to their hunting grounds.

Some distance still separated the two groups.

Words were few in the shoal. The salmon concentrated on their own efforts and the crossing of the border between river and sea, between saltwater and fresh.

Freda looked around. She saw dissolution. The school was further strung out. Fish were being defined by the power with which they could urge themselves forwards. It marked a stark contrast to the tight, marshalled drive she had led from out of the destruction of the whale's wake all that time ago.

The salmon were increasingly scattered across the water. Fragments, connected by loose threads, criss-crossing the breaking tide.

Swimming against the current, salivating, happy, the sea lions hacked away at the distance that kept them from their food.

Freda was still close to Elu. Leith was near as well, slightly in front.

Despite the growing changes in the school's shape, the three of them had agreed, without words or signs, to stay as one.

They were not at the vanguard. Nor were they at the rear.

They could see the leaders ahead of them. Could watch as they scored a line towards the river's mouth.

They could witness as the first sea lions appeared. The sharp head of a hoard marauding through the water, teeth flashing and glinting, glimpsed and then lost.

Slick and strong. How partial that description of the salmon now seemed, when set against the sleek, powerful bodies of the lions. Their smooth, grey skin oiled and illuminated. Their deep, black, bulbous eyes wrapped in puffed up lids. The muscular flex of their bodies as they swam, barely hindered by the tide that worked against them. The sharp swipes of their flippers. The glossy line that curved upwards from the tip of their jaws, along the contours of their rounded heads and then down, in concert with the spine, until it ran out into the wakes left behind by the passage of the beasts through the cool, illumined salt that brooked no favouritism but simply remained, pushing towards the shore and the river's mouth until such a time as that drive would be reversed, as it was daily reversed, and the pendulum would swing in the direction from where it had come.

A bull. The biggest of them all. Father, judge, executioner. Dominance made solid in flesh and teeth and blubber.

Not yet fully grown. Still agile. Still seeking the food that will take him to the edge of his potential. Protein and fat on which to gorge. On which to extend the reach of his body. To gild his power. To threaten. To win.

He rips the water in half. Flippers like roof slates slapping through the salt. His mouth opens, closes. Soft, pink flesh. Hard, yellow blades. Muscles contract and expand across his back. His whole body flexes, jerks under the weight of his immense will.

The first salmon can do nothing as he bears down upon them, his children and his women close behind.

The fish see him. They sense him. But they are in the whip of the tide and the will of their own nature, throwing themselves towards the freshwater with everything they have. No brake can hold them. Their focus is narrow, chiselled to a fine, slender band in which all they can see is the river. It brought them here, to the front of the scattered shoal. It stretched the limits of the group, threatened to break the bonds by which the salmon are bound. Which hold them now, in temporary unity.

They see him. They sense him. It is too late. It was too late before. It is later than that now. It is the time of the bull. It is the time of the end.

They see him. They sense him. They feel the electric punch of the heart, the piston-powered press of the blood speeding inside them.

Twisting, spinning, tearing their bodies upwards in desperate attempts to achieve some impossible braking, they watch as he is upon them. Watch as the swarm of happy, playful sea lions wheel away behind him.

The first one is taken whole. A smaller fish. Swallowed by the bull.

Another. This one larger. Clasped in the jaws. Skin broken. Pain. Blood. Finality. The journey ended. All for naught. No more and no less. An undressed grave, unlabelled and unremarked, here in the water, washed away in moments; scraps of blood and flesh and bone and life subsumed by the salt and its waves.

Freda yells.

She yells like hot steam forcing its way out from beneath a metal lid.

She yells like screeching brakes.

Yells like fire burns.

All of the shoal can see.

Blood is in the water.

Blood of the salmon.

The younger sea lions rise and fall, darting through the crimson cloud, gleeful and excited. The bull shakes his head. Shakes and shakes the half-smashed salmon held between his teeth. Feels the flesh breaking apart. Keeps shaking, whip-snapping his tree-trunk neck until the remains of the fish split in two. Half depart into the salt, float, savaged and bleeding, in the moving water. Half remain, stuck fast within the clamp, haemorrhaging into the sea.

Other salmon are yelling.

Blood is in the water.

Blood of the salmon.

They can taste it. Smell it.

The young sea lions squeal. The bull roars.

The game is on.

Freda dashes upwards, down, left, right. She feels her own blood hammering against the inside of her skin.

Panic in the water. Panic in the salt.

Salmon racing in every direction.

Leith and Elu and Freda trying to stay together. No one following anyone. Everyone following each other.

Lunges, darts, rolls. Squalling fish moving in wild arcs of lash and bend.

Sea lions gamely chasing the prey. Lifting and dropping. Revelling in the pleasure of the hunt. Playing and smiling. Except for the bull. The bull works to a different end.

Freda and Leith and Elu, closer now. Keeping contact. Working for each other. Working for themselves.

Moving forwards. Closing on the river. Travelling down. Seeking the floor. Lion. Lion. Lion. Turning. Rearing up. Muscles straining. Bodies shouting. Fins, tail, face struck by the force of the water. Too quick for the beasts. A break, momentary. Driving again. Three together. Swimming. Swimming. Swimming. The tide rolling above and below and on top. Straining at the edge. Sinews, flanks, scales burning energy. The feeding grounds eroding. Power tapped. Power tapped. The well is sunk and the water is decreasing. Minds narrow into hard, sharp slashes of granite tearing holes through the fabric of the moment, piercing time and shape in search of home. Salt. Fresh. Salt. Fresh. Then and now collapsing into each other. Two bulls rocking back on their haunches. Rolling forwards. Shattering the distance, slapping the flesh, decrying the continuation of two separate forms. There can be only one. Salt or fresh. Salmon or lion. Life or death.

Onwards, onwards they drive. Three salmon bound by the thick ropes of memory, of origin and survival. Onwards. Two sea lions. Young pups. Fattening up through the season. Chasing the fish. Clumsy. Learning. Moving too soon. Moving too fast. Freda, Leith, Elu. Beating, beating, beating their bodies against the water, their fins against the salt, their tails against the wash. Behind them, one of the lions lunging. Mouth wide. Teeth exposed. Fleshy interior salivating in the brine. Snap of the jaw. Short. Again. Short. Chasing, chasing. Black globular eyes transfixed on the fish. Freda breaks.

Spins upwards. Splits the lions. Young pups. One carries on, one rises. The first uncertain, stutters. Turns. Looks at the other. Sees Freda. Leith, Elu lost to view. Driving, Driving. Fresh and salt. Home and past. Closer. Closer. Freda rising. Racing upwards. Two lions. One close, one behind. She pushes. She dies. Dies in the moment. Leaves the sea and the salt and the brine. Returns to the river. Jacob chasing. Jacob beside. Jacob and Freda as one. Soaring, flying, leaping beyond the border. Together. Bound.

She leaves the water. Her silver body is caught in a shimmering cascade of streaming liquid. She is a queen divesting herself of her jewels. A spring sun burning through the fog. An eagle gliding through the air. She soars out of the water, curving herself, bending her body so that tail and head are closer than they have ever been. She sees the land. Sees the salt. Sees the river, waiting, flowing, entering the brine. So close it is. So close.

The lions chase her, flippers thrashing back and forth. They see the water running out in front of them. Feel the light growing stronger. Young pups. Unknowing. Everything the first time. The leader slows, speeds up, slows. The second tries to mimic. Knows nothing but to follow. Slows, speeds up, slows. Out of sync. Seeing then doing. Gains on the other pup. Gains quickly. Tries to slow. Everything the first time. Forgets. Eyes wide; eyes deep. Filled with the edge of the sea, the light. Filled. Blinded by too much. Forgets. Remembers. Tries to slow. Tries to slow. Frantic. Eyes filled. Too fast. Too fast …

*   *   *

As the first sea lion crashed into the back of the second, Freda saw Jacob beside her.

Their bodies were side by side, each curving, each a reflection of the other. Here he was, leaping with her. Here they were, leaping together.

Higher they rose. Higher and higher. The brine sliding from their skins. Streams of water washing off their scales, pouring into the sea. Salt returning to salt.

Freda soared. Felt the sun's heat across her flank. Lived, for a moment, for a lifetime, in the memory she had held, in the ecstasy of escape, from the water, from the world of things, from the sadness and the sorrow; the hope, the joy, the loss.

Freda entered the river, felt herself becoming part of her home. She called in hushed voice. Spoke Jacob's name into the freshwater. Heard him. Heard her name, returning to her through the days and the nights of separation. Heard his voice, his heartbeat. Gripped hold of it. Held it like the mountain holds the earth. Became it. Soared, swam, flew. Knew nothing and everything in the same moment. Grew and shrank. Lived and died. Knew and knew not the meaning of the world in which she moved, of her life, of herself, of Jacob, of all there is and was and evermore will come to be.

Freda, for those few moments beyond the sea, beyond the world that gave her all she had ever had, felt the gentle arms of faith wrap themselves around her once more. Realised how loose those arms had lain across her scales. Saw how close she was. How close the purpose of her life was. Saw with salt-caked eyes the world beyond the self, the world of love. Of extending and inuring oneself in the protection of others; of all that she had done since the first days of the sea. Of all that she would do in the days ahead. Of all that she had been put here to do. Of all that she and Jacob would have done together if they could, but that she had done alone, for him; as he would have done, she knew, for her, had done for her, wherever he was. Of all that was left for her to do, for him, for herself, for those who were still to come, the kin as yet unborn, forever awaited, forever loved.

*   *   *

She hit the water, dived, spat fire through her body, whipped it in glorious convulsions of freedom and return.

Felt herself renewed. Passed through the remaining licks of salt. Tore towards the river.

Behind her, the sea lions tumbled together, pawing at one another. Teeth flashed in brief shows of distaste. Eyes met, grew wide then sharpened. The creatures came

148

close, lashed out as children lash out, unrestrained, without thought.

Freda gave no mind to what was behind her. Ahead lay the river. So near now.

The brine was losing the battle. It was ceding ground, being pushed back to the boundary, the invisible line that marked the transition from one world to another.

Salmon were scattered across the water. They swam in front of her, to the side, above, below. The sea lions, who continued to feed and hunt and play in the deeper salt, had cleaved the shoal apart.

Images of Leith and Elu pressed into her mind, fighting for space.

She felt herself at the edges of the tide's long breaths. Sensed the changing movements of the water. Torque and stretch and swirl.

Upon the boundary she lost control, misjudging the nature of the flow. Her head dipped; her body rolled to one side. She stuck out a fin, flexed her tail. The webs of skin broke her speed, but only a little. She kept spinning. Every anchor was lost. Streams of bubbles blurred her vision. She flexed harder, felt force running through her spine, working against her.

Something struck her side.

A sharp, heavy smack.

She bucked, slapped her body through the water in the direction of the spin, cracked her tail up and down, thrust herself forwards without knowing what direction forwards was.

Aching muscles asked her to stop. Energy was seeping from her flanks.

The bubbles subsided. She was travelling upwards, towards the water's surface. The river was ahead of her.

Breathing hard, she righted herself.

Two systems were clashing, neither minded to buckle. The tide stalked the land as the river entered the sea. Both pushed, both pressed. The border was a mass of indecision, the problems of liquid mechanics played out to swirling resolution.

Freda struggled to grasp the change.

The river was hers. Only the far edge of the boundary left to break. But the river would not help her. It fought against her. Pushed back. Presented her with an obstacle, at once so obvious and yet one that she had never had cause to consider.

She redoubled her efforts, felt her body nudging forwards, heard the water rushing past.

Other salmon were struggling too. Across the estuary, they were clashing with the flow of the river, straining their fins and muscles and tails to break free of the brine and begin moving upstream.

One, two, three fish went quickly past her. Large males, propelling themselves through the water with great slashes and whips.

Somehow, others from the school had caught up and were overtaking.

Still kicking her way through the water, she saw another and then another come by.

Her body was starting to become accustomed to the new equilibrium. It did not call out so loudly, began to bend more easily to her will.

But it did not make sense, she thought. How could salmon from what remained of the shoal have made up the space in such short time? How could they have cast aside the carnage caused by the attack of the sea lions?

She kept swimming, battling the current. Water rushed into her as she tacked a line through the unrelenting flow.

In front, the salmon were branching off left and right. They were making for the river's edges. Perhaps in belief that some respite would be afforded there. Perhaps to follow the river's line more easily. Perhaps because someone had moved and, among the hard struggle of the drive, others had assumed, unthinking, that there was purpose there, that someone knew a way to make this easier.

More fish came past Freda. They hurtled along, tails flashing.

She looked ahead. Saw that she would have to decide. Left, right or alone.

There had been enough alone for a lifetime. She would choose one or the other.

Through the roaring current she looked, straining to distinguish between each side. Leith and Elu dashed through her mind. How she wanted to choose the half to which they belonged.

Another fish came by.

It sailed close to her face, its tail passing within a fin's width.

She flinched, drew away, turned her head.

For a moment she was looking backwards, into the salt.

Fanning out to one side there was a stream of salmon. It was not the shoal with which she had come. These fish were another group. They were moving through the shifting water beneath the waves, using this as a route through which to track the shore and slingshot themselves into the river's mouth.

Every sense, every cell, every ounce of energy inside Freda's body begged her not to turn away. All of it called to her, asking her to stay facing in this direction, looking into the new source of fellow salmon; these fish who had come from elsewhere. Who could be anybody or anyone, except for the fact that they were of the river, just like her, just like Leith, Elu and all the others with whom she had crossed half the world in search of return. In search of home.

Jacob.

But she knew she had to keep moving. So much depended on it. There was no time. Oh! How there had been time in the years that had passed. Time enough to sink an empire and raise a steeple to the skies. And yet now, when time was all she wanted, there was none to which she could lay claim.

Turning, she took her chance and moved left, braking with one fin while pushing hard with the other.

*   *   *

Night hung across the river. The two groups rested among different reeds. Freda's group were higher up, though they did not know it. Not one fish from either side had caught sight of the others following the split.

Marks of decay were beginning to appear in the rich, oiled skins of the salmon. There had been no food since the feeding grounds. Beaten by the swell and flow of the river, the fish waited in silence, the first signs of their waning power made flesh. Some slept, some passed between lucidity and the deep silence of exhaustion, flickering like a candle's flame.

Freda was awake. She was tired, yes, but awake. Sleep would not come. It waited somewhere else, far off, beyond the river and the sea, beyond even the air and the sun that she had known three times now. It would come, she knew, further along the river's bend. It would have to. But not tonight. Not now.

She looked at her fellow salmon. Saw Leith sleeping next to Elu. Exhaled in relief as she returned to the memory of seeing them in the river's flow, of the delight she had felt, of the confirmation she had found, confirmation that this time her choice had led her towards and not away.

Salmon filled the space around her. She could see the early damage to their scales, knew that if she could look, she would see the same marks written upon the surface of her own body. The marks that spoke the story's end.

How different the river seemed. Different to memory. Different to expectation, to the illustrated tales of hope and redemption told daily in the minds of the fish. In Freda's mind. In the inner world she had built over the years of absence. Carved and hewn and made with words and deeds, thoughts and wishes. A world shot through with faith, with certainty. One in which she had sat and waited for so many days, so many months, so many heartbeats.

And now, now that they were here, adults swimming in the fin-swipes of children, how different the river seemed.

It was smaller. Or, at least, they were larger. It did not taste as she remembered. It did not smell the same. There was the echo of what she knew, but it ran beneath that which was.

A brief longing for the hard sharpness of the salt escaped her, an unmarked breath she never dreamed would leave her lips.

No longer was this the water of their birth. That time had passed. So too had the river they had known. This was a different river, every element replaced, every drop that flowed against them a reminder of time's quick passage.

And, Freda wondered, even though the days ahead would feel like months, as the salmon battled the current, fought their way home, stymied at every step by the flow, the rage, the power of the driving water, how much time had they left? How much more was there to this journey, this pilgrimage on which they had set out in the very first moments of their birth, following in the wakes and trails of their ancestors?

And she knew, as we all know, that time is where we live, that all that lives so too must die; that the clock signals the strong, beating pulse of life just as it signals the hastening of our days; that the fire that burns, burns for us all. And that when those moments of transition come, those seconds in which the clock stops for some and starts for others, in those brief hours, those softening taps of the drum, we know the passing of one flame is accompanied by the rising of another, that the fire that has burned for us has burned with all its might and power, giving light and heat to the world, bringing warmth where cold could have spread, bringing light where darkness could have risen, bringing something where nothing might have been. She knew this, Freda. Knew it as the salt knows the sea. Knew it as the moon knows the night. As the mother knows the child.

Perhaps Jacob was here, she thought, thinking these same things. Waiting elsewhere, like her. On the other side of the river, perhaps, further up, somewhere behind. Or maybe he was not here yet, and his story had further to go – another season in the feeding grounds, an entrance to the estuary less fraught – before he too passed on, both himself and his lineage, the same as her.

As she waited there, in that dark night, Freda knew many things. She resolved that she would know them until her job was done. That, no matter what awaited, she would hold them tight and close. And in those things that she knew, there was the light and the dark, the warmth and the cold, the river and the sea. And there was Jacob. And beneath it all, there was love.

Part Seven – Journey's End

'Have you had anything to eat?'

'I don't think there's much around here.'

'It was some eating back in those feeding grounds, wasn't it?'

'There were days when it felt like all the food in the sea was there, just waiting to be eaten. All for us. Everything we could ever want.'

'I'm so hungry.'

'You won't make it any better by thinking about it.'

'I can't help it,' said Leith. 'It's thinking about me. My stomach's sending out rescue signals. It's desperate. Needs help. Listen. Can you hear it?'

Freda and Elu laughed.

'Everyone's hungry. Maybe there'll be something to eat further up.'

'Really?' said Leith, his voice flattening. 'You think so?'

'She's just saying, Leith.'

'Just saying … Well, I doubt it. If there was decent food in the river we'd never have left.'

He moved away.

'The river's changed since we were here. Maybe there's food now.'

'You never know. There might be something for us to eat, Leith. Could be just around the corner.'

He swam back and came to a stop in front of them.

'The river hasn't changed. It's the same as it ever was. There isn't any food here and there isn't going to be any food further up. We've had our fill. All we've got left is fighting and dying until we get home and then, if we even make it, we'll do what we need to do, and all this will be over.'

He cast a fin out in an arc, signalling the world that encompassed them.

'I'm hungry and I'm going to be hungry for the rest of my life, however long that is.'

He glared at them.

'Correction, we'll all be hungry for the rest of our lives. Not just you.'

He let out a snort of irritation. Bubbles burst through the water.

'You should make the most of this, Leith.'

He looked at Freda, cocked his head.

'It isn't going to get any better. You'll soon be hungrier than you are now.'

'This is probably the least hungry you'll be,' said Elu. 'Right now. Here.'

She pointed a fin at the riverbed.

'You should enjoy it, Leith. We all should,' said Freda.

'That's right,' said Elu. 'This is like a holiday. It's not going to get better than this.'

Leith scowled, turned and buzzed his tail at them. He swam a few feet away, stopped and came back.

'I'm so hungry,' he said. 'My stomach's groaning. It needs to be fed. I need to be fed. I want food.'

Freda and Elu laughed, gently.

'It's not going to get any better, but you might get used to it.'

'When we set off, you'll have something else to think about. You'll be distracted.'

'Distracted … The only thing that's distracting me is the thought of all those salmon still out there in those grounds, stuffing their faces with every last thing they can get hold of.'

Leith groaned, devastated by the thought.

'Come on,' said Freda. 'Chin up. We'll be alright. You'll see.'

*   *   *

The group of salmon sets off. It is early morning. White clouds range across the sky. Light mixes with the last dregs of darkness. Dew hangs from grass and bushes. Across the land, creatures are waking.

Wide and powerful, the river dominates life. We are a few miles inland, away from the estuary but still within the flats, those level planes that tip ever so slightly seaward, draining the river, fostering abundance.

A gamut of fresh greens coat the landscape, broken by slivers of brown and specks of colour.

Ripples and waves map the river's surface, a vast swathe of rolling hills, shifting and changing as the water flows towards the salt, pulled by the forces of the earth, called by the vast expanse of the seas.

Light spits and runs across the liquid, dipping, rising, glinting, scattering.

Beneath the surface we see shapes. Shadows. Moving in pairs, threes, groups. A contingent of émigrés returning home, loosely bound, letting the bonds of exile weaken as their purpose wanes, eroded by the growing knowledge that all was not in vain. And yet, the return plays out other than expected. Inside the river the salmon are outsized. Already they look like giants stalking the paths that guide them home. They will grow bigger the further they travel, bludgeoning through the water as the river narrows.

They are adults walking in woods where monsters once roamed, where castles were built and treasures found. They are subjects seeing their portraits decades hence, recognising the paint and the lines and the shapes, but recognising too all that has been lost, all that has been gained.

We see the shadows pushing against the flow. We see the slide and roll, the shifting lines, the search for wakes, for currents more favourable, for respite, for breath.

We see nothing but the salmon. We see them, bound into their lives, encompassed by the water, grown and aged and worn. We see them, wise and experienced, set on their mission, struggling, winning, tasting defeat and then clearing the flavour from their mouths, casting loss outside of themselves until they are ready to forge on once more, marine Sisyphus's pushing their boulders against the current, watching as hope and power come to naught over and again in the face of suffering and forbearance, stopping, waiting, for a moment, resetting themselves in their unending task of returning the rock to the mountain's peak.

We see life making itself known to the world, battling against the elemental forces of the universe, decrying gravity, calling out all that might stand in opposition to the electric fires of animation, the soft, coursing heat of being, the answer to every question, writ large on the skins and the scales, even now, as they flake and fold and founder beneath the torrent, breaking apart as their energy is ever more depleted, expended in response to the songs of the species, sung in the minds and bodies of every salmon who ever emerged into the water and the light, spent in knowing search of the grounds from which life springs, from which it sprang for them and from which it will come again for all those who follow.

We see the story's end foretold in the shimmering skins of the fish. We see the beginning too, the beginning of another journey, the start of something known to all of those who live already, who have breathed the breath of life. An eternal origin reimagined again and again and again, every time cast as new, carved from the echoes and the memories and the senses and the souls of those for whom the day has reached its end, for whom night is calling, for whom life is a flame to be passed on, such that it might burn more brightly than before, in the hands of those who will forge the world anew, for whom the bell tolls in soft, muffled tones. A toll that extracts no vengeance, that brings no penance, shames no guilt or fear from those that hear it. A toll that reminds, that gilds the edges of a shadow long known. A toll that names all that we have done, that holds our lives to the skies and gives us solace. A toll that darkens the water, bringing into clear focus every last drop of light that falls around us, shines within us, snaps and cracks and fizzes through our veins. A toll that took the salmon to the sea and brought them back again, that gave them life and hope and love, that staunched the wounds in times of despair, that asked the question to which each day is an answer.

We see

We see

We see

* * *

'I'll have to rest soon.'

Leith's skin had lost its lustre. He looked old. He looked sad.

'Let's keep going a little longer.'

'There's a bend a bit further ahead if I remember right. We can rest on the inside of that.'

'You don't know it's there.'

'Alright, Leith. I'm pretty sure it's there. Things keep coming back to me.'

'The longer we wait before stopping, the better.'

'I agree. Let's wait till we get round that bend, at least.'

'I can't wait. I need to rest.'

'You'll have to wait,' Freda said, 'because we're not leaving you and we're not stopping. Not yet, anyway.'

She released some of the tension in her fins and slipped back through the current. Braking hard she slowed and then began to move forward again, wriggling her body through the fast-moving water.

'Keep this speed up and we'll be there soon enough,' she said, her head level with Leith's.

Elu remained in front.

'Stick with him, Freda. We'll take it in turns if we need to.'

Leith let out a sigh.

'What a way to end up,' he said.

'I think you ate too much,' said Freda, smiling, her body aching from the river's onslaught.

' … '

Freda laughed.

Elu joined in.

'You ate too much,' she shouted back. 'Now you're so big you can't get through the water. There's too much of you to carry. You're working against yourself!'

'Should've stayed slim and agile like me and Elu. All that food was too easy for you. Laid out on a plate like that.'

Leith smiled despite himself. He started to laugh.

'Oh, I wish I had all that food in front of me now. I'd get so big you wouldn't even be able to fit me in this river. I'd eat and eat and eat until I was as big as a whale.' He paused, got his breath back. 'Leith the whale-salmon they'd call me, and I'd never come home. I'd never come back to this damn river. I'd just swim around the salt, eating and eating and eating. All day long'

'Big salmon make a tasty catch.'

'Big salmon get fat and slow!'

Leith shrugged.

'Fat and slow is better than hungry.'

'Well, you're not fat and slow yet, so keep going and we'll have a rest when we get round that bend.'

Leith winced as pieces of silt whipped up by the current caught in the open wounds on his back.

'That magic bend, oh yes,' he said. 'Is there any chance you can recall it being a bit closer? Perhaps it's actually just here and you've suddenly remembered. Then we could stop and have a rest.'

The water rushed past them.

In front and behind small groups of salmon were strung along the water's path. A few fish travelled on their own, though most had joined pods. Memories of the great shoals and schools of the sea.

Every fish was bleeding energy into the river, trying to fill an appetite insatiable.

Some dipped and rose, attempting to carve a path beneath the main push of the current.

Others bore on, straight and true, resolved to their lot, unwilling to risk the steadiness they craved; unconvinced that more would triumph over less should they leave the line they had found.

Freda dropped back a touch, so that she was level with Leith's tail. Here she could see how badly he was faring. Slivers of scale hung from all over his body.

*   *   *

It was night again. They rested near the bank, camouflaged by vegetation. This time Freda slept.

Each day was an exercise in suffering. There was no respite. Every one of them was fighting the river. For all that they moved in pods or groups, in trysts of friendship like Freda, Elu and Leith, the final leg of the journey was a personal torment for each fish. A silent requiem in which the only voice was their own and the only instrument was the rushing water of the river.

Freda's body was degrading. She could feel the softening of her skin, the opening of small wounds, the diminishing power of her muscles.

Her mind, though, was strong.

Moving through the current during the long days, she saw the many salmon that moved as they did. In their shape and form she saw hope. Hope that Jacob might be among them. That he too was travelling home, swimming along the path they had shared for that brief time. Time that, as it was lived, had felt like centuries, days and nights stretched out as far as they would go, each second glowing and burning against the senses.

After night came morning. Leith regained a little of his bonhomie. Freda watched as he set off, following Elu's lead. She saw a friend denuded, a canvas being slowly cleared of paint. Wondered, briefly, if the same could be said of her.

Days went past. The friends pushed further up the river, gaining inch after inch in hard fought, draining fin-slashes. They flexed their bodies, whipped their tails, gritted their teeth.

All the way they remained alone and yet surrounded. Other salmon mirrored their efforts. Silver, brown, orange bodies pockmarked by decay and portents of decline. Each one battling the river. Driven towards its goal. Unbending.

Some, though, did fall.

Freda was taking her turn at the front. Leith was in the middle, Elu behind.

The river was narrower. Gone was the wide expanse afforded by the flatlands. Here, the terrain rose, beginning the ascent that would take it, eventually, beyond the birthing grounds of the salmon and up into the mountain peaks, to the source of the river and then higher still, to the places where life was but a shallow breath, a quiet noise, hard to perceive.

With the steepening land there came a faster flow. Gravity pulled hard.

Space was not yet at a premium, as it would be further up, but the lessening volume was challenging the salmon to think and watch more carefully.

In this fluctuating world, where the fish's minds were pulled at the same time as their bodies were pushed, the threat was greater, enlarged by the joint demands of thought and movement.

Ahead of them, to the left, not far from the bank, halfway between the bed and the surface, a fish, swimming alone, tail slapping back and forth, skin dull and broken, stuttered in the current.

An eddy, swirling, cutting across the general flow of the water, unhinged it from its path.

The salmon's tail worked in a diagonal. It thrust out a fin, beat it wildly up and down.

Freda saw the fish move backwards, saw it twist and turn, trying to fight the pressure.

Another movement. This one pushing it closer to the bank.

The salmon slashed in the water, lost balance and was turned over by the current. It spun, swirled, fell downstream.

Freda watched as it neared.

A shot of mud and dust billowed into the river as the fish crashed into the bank.

Freda braked, bore right, pushed hard against the current.

The water thickened, darkened, as the brown plume diffused.

A noise. A long-remembered noise. The eagle. A screech, a yell. Fear fleshed out and voiced.

Freda came through the cloud, darted a look behind. She saw Leith, saw Elu, began to breathe again. Saw the muddied water. Impenetrable. A churning fog denying the presence of the fish who fell. Separating Elu and Leith and Freda from their past, recent and old.

Ahead lies another past. Ancient and sleeping, ready to awaken once more.

*   *   *

'I ate something today,' said Leith.

Freda and Elu did not respond. They were still, resting in a deep dip beside the bank. A dip familiar to them. One in which they had rested before.

'I'm sure of it. I saw it in the current and I opened my mouth and I grabbed it. Food. The first food in ages. Maybe there'll be more tomorrow. This could be where things change,' he said, his eyes bright, staring upstream, past his friends, into the darkness.

'What do you think, Freda?' asked Elu.

Freda shrugged.

'I think it's near.'

She did not respond.

'It must be. This place is familiar. You know that.'

Freda let herself rise a little higher in the water.

'If there's food tomorrow, I'm going to go all out for it. You'll see. Anything that comes, it's mine. You two shouldn't even try eating it. I need it, you see. Need to get this body of mine in good condition again. We might get back out to sea, you know. Might have enough to go back, after we've reached home. I've heard stories. Some salmon make it. There were ones at the feeding grounds. Said they'd been there and back plenty of times. That could be us. Me, definitely. You'll have to see how you get on. Any food tomorrow is mine. Don't forget that. I have to eat. Got to have enough to make it back.'

His voice trailed off.

'Why don't you try to get some sleep, Leith?' said Freda. 'We'll see if there's any food tomorrow.'

Leith looked at her. For a moment, he wondered who she was.

'There'll be food alright,' he said. 'Food for everybody. But mostly for me. I can taste it. Had some today. That was a sign.'

He yawned.

'I'm tired … I need to sleep a long time. Got to get ready. There's a lot to get ready. A lot of things. There'll be food tomorrow. Got to be ready for it.'

He was whispering, the words washing gently from his mouth. As the last one tumbled across his jaw his eyes dimmed.

Freda turned her head. She had been following Leith's gaze, looking into the narrowing, blackened depths ahead of them.

She drew herself next to Elu.

'We're close,' she said.

*   *   *

The next morning, when they awoke, Leith was dead.

His weak, damaged body floated upside down, skin ravaged, eyes open, staring back in the direction of the sea, scales leaden and grey, mouth agape, tail caught beneath a thick root that crawled along the bank.

Neither of them spoke.

They moved towards him. Elu brushed a fin along his back. Freda swam to his tail, used her head to press the root.

Elu joined her, helped.

After a few minutes they worked him free.

For a moment, he was still, the world turned upside down, resting beside them. Then he was gone, taken by the current, lifted toward the surface, carried away, downstream, towards the salt.

On either side of the river, other salmon were waking, tired and decaying, ready to resume their slow journeys.

Freda and Elu waited a while.

A few small fry came past them.

'Food,' said Elu.

And they set off, the two of them, forging on in the face of it all. As they had always done. As they would always do.

Two shaded shapes beneath the water. Each shadowed by a second form. The mark of absence, emptying them once more as they swam on, fighting and fighting for that which called to them. For life. For Leith.

*   *   *

Leith's reverie turned out to be prophetic.

There was food here, in these higher reaches of the river.

The water was cooler, the path narrower and not as deep.

Still there was enough room for the salmon to travel with relative ease, but they had to adapt their movements to the water's changing form. None of them now rose and fell in search of the path of least resistance. All attended to the changing shapes of bed and bank, wary, lest they be undone by the unexpected.

Freda and Elu ate whatever they could.

It brought them renewed strength, stirring their minds and feeding their bodies.

They pushed on, Freda leading, guiding her friend, thinking of Leith, of Jacob.

She knew, deep down, beneath the surface, that time was running out.

She had hoped they would come across him as they rose with the river, perhaps catching him up, perhaps seeing him swim past them, upon which they would have called and he would have turned and together they would have seen each other, would have been reunited after the years of loss and hope and waiting.

But it had not come to pass.

Leith's death had warned them both. Reminded them of how far they had come, how near they were and, yet, how much still stood between them and the ending they sought.

For Freda, it had cast open the wound inside of her, the one that she had worked so hard to hold and to heal, knowing all the while that only one thing would be enough to truly make it whole again.

Now the water was falling fast. Up ahead they could see splash and foam and bursts of bubbles.

'I remember,' said Freda, speaking half to herself and half to Elu, who was struggling a few feet behind, engaged in her own monologue, urging herself not to stop.

Freda slowed, fell level with her friend.

She turned, began to speak, saw the pain in Elu's eyes.

' … '

The words caught in her throat.

'It'll never end, will it, Freda?'

Her voice was cracked and dry; it scraped along her throat, rattled around the base of her mouth.

'We've made it this far, haven't we? We can make it a bit further. That's all it'll take it. I'm sure of it.'

'I don't want to make it without Leith,' she said, barely audible as her voice squeaked and wheezed.

Freda steeled herself, felt the fire of doubt rising inside, doused the flames.

'We're doing it for all of us,' she said. 'You're doing it for me and I'm doing it for you. We're doing it because they did it for us. We're doing it because we can, and we will.'

Elu sobbed.

Freda moved closer to her, touched a fin against her side.

'There's a fall ahead.'

Elu looked at her, shook the tears from her eyes.

All the while, the two salmon were still swimming, still pressing themselves forwards through the flow.

'Up ahead. There's a fall. Remember? Where the river drops. We swam through it when we left. Hardly noticed, I suppose, because it was so easy. Just another couple of fin-beats in the current. It'll be a lot harder this time.'

A stronger current seized them, rocked them to one side, threw up a gap between them.

Freda tried to move back, to get closer to Elu again, found herself repelled by the water.

She looked across, saw Elu struggling in the flow.

'Keep going!' she shouted.

She could not tell if Elu heard her.

'Jump,' she yelled, water smashing into her, blinding her, rocking her this way and that, demanding more and more from her tail, her fins, her flanks.

'Jump! The fall. You'll have to jump it!'

Haphazard currents cut and sliced, whipped up by the crashing vortex beneath the waterfall. The drop stood several feet high. High enough to add weight and pace to the water's flow. High enough to loom above the approaching salmon.

Freda clawed at the water. Her body bent and stretched. She hacked her tail, dragging it this way and that. She saw salmon in front of her. They were diving, their tails sticking upwards, in the direction of the surface.

Heart racing, sight coming and going as washes of bubbles fell across her eyes, as she strained her body, pushing, pushing, pushing against the river, she tried to call out to Elu.

' … '

No breath was free. All was flowing into the river and the fight.

She was moving forwards, closer to the diving fish.

Again she tried to call.

Again she failed.

The water was uncontrolled, unbidden.

It whipped and ran and shot and darted in every direction, a short, brief interlude within the unbending will of the river.

Another salmon dived in front of her.

She saw it falling, pulling up, pulsing towards the surface.

She followed, without thought or question.

There was a depression. The force of the water, exerted since before time could be counted in cycles of fish, since before it could be numbered off against the charts and tables of men and women, had cracked the riverbed, creating a deep pool into which the salmon were throwing themselves, such that they might slingshot upwards and break the angry, fizzing surface of the waterfall.

Freda fell towards the floor. She felt herself gaining speed, threw out her fins, cracked her tail and winced as her body shouted in pain, begging her to retreat.

Now she was rising, accelerating, closing in on the river's edge.

Freedom.

Respite.

Momentary.

Brief.

The water below her, the journey, the pain, the suffering, hope and doubt, the faith and forgiveness, the long, hard days of travel, the salt and the fresh water, the feeding grounds, the friends, the time, the days, the seconds, the ebb and flow of life, the love that girded it all, that ran through everything like light runs through the dawn; the thoughts, the senses, the group and the solitude; the striving, the persistence; the adversity, the closeness, the distance; those who had gone, those who remained, those over whom the question hung; Lox and Elu, Leith and Stephen. Those who had left. Those who were leaving. Those who were and those who would. Herself. Jacob. These last few days of love.

*   *   *

Freda flew through the air, her careworn body flashing specks of orange and silver, dregs of oil and lustre still present in patches of effervescence that shone and glinted in the sunlight, proud defiance standing firm in flecks and slivers hidden within the beleaguered scales.

In front of her was the river, twisting and flowing across the land. She could see two more jumps ahead. She could see familiar places. Memories returned to flesh.

Another fish, larger than her, came past, leaping higher and further. For a moment they were side by side, leaping as one.

Her heart jumped, left her chest and soared towards the heavens.

The fish bent in the air, began to fall, heading for the river.

It was not him.

Freda crashed into the freshwater. Frantically thrashing, feeling the pull of the waterfall behind her, she battled the flow.

Something wasn't right.

A smell.

A taste.

Known but rare, conjuring something from inside. A feeling. A hurt not long recognised. Pain. Fear.

Her head was racing. It bounced and whirled, switching from ecstasy to lament. She could not fix her attention on what was wrong. Jacob ran across her mind, the first time they had leapt, those memories, red-hot, fire-cracking life coursing beneath their skin. So close now, so close. And then Elu, where was she? Had she leapt? But so far left. And still Jacob was not here. And still her faith was not revealed as truth. And still more forbearance to come. Two more jumps. Her body so tired, weakened, so pained.

Pushing through the water, Freda felt herself fading in and out of the present.

She was here, in the river, old and weary, closing on the goal, alone and tired.

She was here, in the river, young, innocent, tearing through the water, chasing Jacob, dipping and rising in his wake.

She was in the estuary, making her choice, the wrong choice, but so too the one that had brought her back, carried her thousands of miles through worlds she could never have imagined.

She was in the salt, inside the sea, inside the whale, rising from the depths, pressing her giant grey, silken body through the water, breaking the surface, crashing into the waves.

She was in the feeding grounds, Stephen leaving her, she leaving him, the two of them leaving each other.

She was in the shoal, returning home.

She was in the border, between salt and fresh, inside the sea lions, inside the blood and the broken bodies.

Blood.

Her chest contracted.

Blood.

Her muscles winced.

Blood in the water.

A giant paw burst into the river, swung through the flow and tried to grab hold of her.

A second paw landed behind. Shockwaves. The current disrupted. Swirls and eddies. Thrusts of bubbles. Shrieks. Blood: taste it, smell it. Salt.

She banked right, felt a claw scratch along her side, lashed her tail and surged through the bear's grasp.

It tried again, fell forward, juddering into the water.

She dipped left, moved down, up, right and down again.

The bear waved its paw through the liquid, chasing her, one step behind, slow and cumbersome. Violent. Hungry.

She flayed her fins, flexed her body, called up all the energy she still possessed. Zigzagged through the river.

Water screamed in her ears. Blood crept onto her tongue, bitter and metallic and salted.

She glanced up. The bear was moving. A brown shadow. A lumbering giant, tracing the riverbank.

All thoughts, all memories, all concerns of then and now and just before were wiped from her mind.

Only the bear and the river remained.

She saw it stop. Watched as it grew in size. Kept on fighting. Kept driving and driving against the flow. Flicked her head and looked again. Saw the shadow rearing up to the outer limits of the world, casting itself into a mountain. A flesh and blood, teeth and claw reimagining of rock and scree, peak and crag.

Whipping her tail to one side she steered away from the bank, dived deeper, cut across the current, felt herself treading water, turned straight again, ploughed into the flow, further from the edge now, deeper again.

The mountain collapsed, erupted in a landslide, arms, head, paws crashing through the surface of the river.

A jaw, spread wide, dark flesh pierced by two half rings of white, iron fangs, pink tongue slithering across the bottom line, castled on either side by canines, sharpened screwdrivers rising above the low roofs of knives and scalpels, inches from Freda's face, close enough to breathe its heat onto her, to pull her gaze, fleetingly, into the abyss, to speak in roaring voice the final, harsh cessation of all things, to name this moment as journey's end.

The jaws snapped shut.

        *   *   *

It was a young bear. Immature. Excitable.

What paroxysms of delight had exploded in its mind when it sighted the river, stocked full of large, fat fish, swollen by their time at sea, struggling to make their way upstream, blocked and buffeted by the water's flow.

How it had bounded across the grass, barely able to contain itself, haunches bouncing, head bobbing, slaver dripping from its mouth.

On reaching the bank it had stopped and stared into the water as elation rose through its vast limbs, tough, powerful muscles and bushy brown coat.

The larder was full. The wait had been repaid. The struggle, the atonement, was not in vain. Nature had provided.

But not just yet.

Freda was damned if she was going to let it finish here.

She was damned if she was going to meet her end at the hands of another, not when she was this close. Not when she had swum halfway across the world and back, survived, led, prospered, risen and fallen a hundred times, tasted the bittersweetness of love and loss – the two sides of the same coin, the two syllables of the same word, the two halves of the same whole.

And she was damned if she was going to fall short, if she was going to let this monster intrude on her ascent to the birthing grounds, to the purpose for which she had been born, for which she had been raised, in which she had believed and had faith since those first fire-filled moments of life, when the flame-hot crackles of being had electrified her soul, burgeoned inside her nascent body, driven her into the world and the universe and all the undulating echoes of sense and feeling.

Down she went, into the well of her belief, her own abyss, the depths of faith that she could never fully plumb, in which she found no walls and touched no bottom. She swam as deep as she had ever dared to travel, shooting through the space like the river racing to the sea.

With every slash of the fin, every flick of the tail, she summoned the remnants of what she had left, called to the edges of her world, drew the outer limits of all she knew toward herself.

Her body moved like she had never known it to move.

Every muscle wrenched in unison. Fierce energy hurtled beneath her skin. It deafened her, roaring through each last inch of flesh.

She leapt out of the water, saw the bear's thick body, his head still stuck in the river.

She smashed back into the flow, rode it, powered forwards, her whole form flexing as one, sending her upstream, tearing the water apart, rocketing her through the current.

Before she knew what was happening, she was out of the flow, leaping again, piercing the river's surface, rising into the air, arcing down, re-entering the water, dipping through the current, propelling herself past other fish, past the lengths of the bank, far away from the clamp of hungry, grizzled jaws.

Once more she leapt. By now she was close to the second fall. It was shallower than the last, but not the lowest of the three.

That distinction was reserved for the final one, that she could see, a little further ahead, midway along a bend, dotted with a family of bears, led by a mother who was older, wiser and who knew where to wait for the easiest catch.

She reached the second fall, threw herself out of the river, climbed and climbed, through the air, over the cascading water, beyond the ledge, past the foam and froth, closer to her goal, closer to the last, single obstacle that stood between her and the end. Stood between her and the world in which she had been born. Between her and the home she and Jacob had made their own.

Fish struggled around her. Salmon intent on the same mission as Freda. Focussed and anxious, willing themselves on, tired, wracked by decay, fading slowly, half-formed into remembrances of what once had been.

Elu, Jacob, flashed across her mind.

She saw Leith's dead body floating down the river, carried towards her by the unyielding current, that permanent aggressor that would not relent, chip, chip, chipping away second after second, minute after minute, driving back towards the salt.

She saw Elu swimming beside her, staring ahead, vacant, eyes hollow and remote.

She saw Jacob, beckoning her, racing in front, leaving the water, returning, coming up to her, planting a kiss upon her lips, smiling, falling, falling, falling.

A scream stabbed through the water's swell.

Blood. Thicker this time. Stronger.

A splash. Something entering the river, picked up by the current, thrown towards her.

She dived left, swung her body out of the way.

A red trail marking the water, diffusing, tinting the clear liquid, throwing its rich blush across the flow.

She leapt again, threw herself into the air, looked ahead, marked the position of the bears, saw her kin, some dying, some dead; some passing on, slipping, gliding, sailing past the dripping beasts.

Back in the river. Still fighting. The last vestiges of energy flashing inside. Burning the underneath of her skin. Shouting in her ears. Mixing with the current, with memories, with here and then and now and was and is and will.

She jumped.

She leapt.

She flew.

Her trajectory was low. She tacked right inside the water, exited the flow near to the bank. As she soared, the bears were away from her, stood waiting on the ledge, water rushing between their legs, their fur wet and heavy, specks of liquid dripping back into the river. They waited expectantly, watching, opening their mouths, leaning forward, catching hold of a body, a tail, a head.

She flew.

They saw her. They did not move. Why move? There was food enough. Untold salmon were trying to reach their homes; more were still to come.

They saw her; she saw them. She watched as she travelled, her mind swimming, submerged within the deep, testing waters of the journey and by this, the waiting fate that she was avoiding, to which others succumbed as she looked, to which more would fall in the days and weeks that followed; Elu? Jacob?

She flew.

*   *   *

Two more days of struggle. No bears here. They have their spot, passed on from mother to child.

An old place, this. Small and shallow. Not like the river. Not like the sea. An old place, once known. Lived in when it was large and deep. Light dapples the surface, passes down to the bed, illumines the clear, clean water that feeds the banks and the birds and the beasts, that births the fish, nourishes them, sustains them.

An old salmon in an old place. Freda is weaker than she has ever been. Alone. Close to unrecognised kin who twitch and flick and swim.

She waits. Looks out, half-heartedly, for food. Mouths at scraps and insects. Motor movements, nothing more. Partial. Incomplete.

Death is here.

Life is here.

The floating remnants of newly-dead salmon mix with those fish who are just arriving and those for whom breath is short and shallow, whose skins have all but faded.

Nests dot the riverbed. The water flows quickly. Life is growing. Roe and milt fused together.

Freda's nest is built. She waits above it, passing back and forth, floating on the current, retreating upstream, floating again.

She looks downriver, lapses into sleep, wakes, questions herself, counts the days by the sunlight's rise and fall.

Three days she counts.

On each one she weakens. The fight here is not the same. There is no pursuit to animate it. All is finished. The goal is the goal is the goal. And the goal has been fulfilled.

She counts. Three days she counts. The sun rises. The sun falls. All the world continues, ignorant of Freda Salmon, and the vigil that she keeps.

But here, in this old place, there is every part of the world. There is life. There is death.

In those three days, Freda sees it. She sees the light wane beneath the torn, ripped surfaces of the salmon with whom she shares this place.

She sees new life born from the pieces of others, called into being as it has been called again and again across the landscapes of time and space.

She sees herself, emerging into the world. Burning with the fire of life. Electrified by newness, seeking and searching, pressing hard against the boundaries of the possible.

Every moment she has lived returns to her, reimagines itself in the dying embers of her mind. Day and night, start and end, noise and silence.

And in that time, when lucidity arrives and departs, when it comes and goes like footsteps through broken snow, she asks the questions that ride in the vanguard, signalling the coming of the pall: What have I done with these days? What is left of me, when I cease to be? Is this a life, these successions of things that have made me? Is this a life worthy of the name?

And in that time, when lucidity arrives and departs, when it moves like the lamp of a carriage passing through a forest in the dark of night, the answers dip and weave, appear and then dissolve, before the eyes that seek, that ask the dusk, the encroaching clamour of blackening clouds, to speak the words, to name the words, to lay sound upon absence and proclaim in loud voice all that the wait is for. To give the oath that God once gave, to say that all is not in vain; to comfort, to soothe, to calm.

Three days she counts.

One.

Two.

Three.

*　　　　*　　　　*

Freda Salmon is no longer the fish so many knew. She is a shell in which the remains of life rattle and seep. She is a smell that fades, a sound that weakens, a fire that dies.

Three days she counts …

One …

Two …

Three …

*   *   *

And on the fourth day?

There is no fourth day. There is only the third, hacking and spitting into the end.

The third day.

Dark and light and dark again.

There is no fourth day. Only the third, which bleeds across the hours like oil spilt across the sea.

On and on this third day runs, denying the markers of time, enveloping the bell and the tick and the light and the pall in thick, silent smog-belches of flickering blackness.

The third day.

Dark and light and dark again.

Freda, floating and returning. Keeping watch above the empty nest. Fading. Dying.

What can they know of us, Jacob, who only we can know?

But there is no Jacob. There is no salvation here, within the unwitting confines of the river. Here there is only the flow of the water, ceaseless, unminded. Here, in this old place.

There is no fourth day.

Three days she counts …

One …

Two …

Three …

And on the third day, the day in which a thousand days are born and known, in which the world dies, in which it lives; on this day, whichever day it is, this third day, counted by Freda Salmon, a pair of eyes that have seen half the world, lived through pain and chance and love and sorrow, written unread books of hope a hundred times over, lain their gaze upon the lives of others, led the way where no way seemed to beckon, held inside their circles the name and the shape, the sound and the touch of one who loved: on this day, this third day, these eyes fall shut.

*   *   *

One,

Two,

Three …

There is a touch. A push among the flow.

Light creeps into the remnants of Freda's senses. Images play faintly across her mind. She sees a pebble passing on, whipped up by the current.

She feels so heavy. Her eyes turn toward the bed. Her chest sags.

The nest is there. Built. Waiting.

She fades, returns, feels the river as she has never felt it before. Alien. Running across her skin like a creature from a different world.

She feels so heavy. Her eyes are on the bed. Her eyes are on the nest.

One,

Two,

Three …

There is a touch. A push among the flow.

She raises her head, lifts it slowly, feels the open wound on her back, tries to flick her tail, manages barely a swish; moves in feeble judders.

Jacob.

Jacob.

Half-dead.

Skin and scales and flesh.

Grown; changed; alive.

Broken. Whole. Here, in this old place.

Cuts and lesions cover his body. He is weak, breathing in short, narrow breaths.

The nest is there.

One,

Two,

Three …

Jacob.

He moves towards her. She moves towards him. Slow, both of them, tired. They touch. Touch like they have touched every day they've ever lived. Touch like the touch is the breath they pull from the water. Touch like the touch is the river itself, giving life, birthing it, sustaining it.

They live. Live longer than either has the right to live. Live for days, hours, seconds. All time exposed as uncountable, unknowable; undefined and ancient. They live in each other, in the space between. They live in the look and the smell and the touch and the taste. They live in the memories of two lives lived apart, live in the time of the river, in the nascent days upon which two souls set forth as one, bound by bonds that pull like the moon pulls the night, live in the sight and the sound and the voice, live in seconds drawn out to years, live in the tide and the swell, the waves and the heave, the river, the current, the flow.

They live.

One,

Two,

Three …

They live.

Freda. Jacob. Together.

Two halves recast as one. Two lives, no more divergent.

Two souls returned.

And in the milt and the roe of these two souls,

the world, it turns and it turns.

*   *   *

The sun is up. Light falls on the earth. It shimmers and dances across the darting current of the river. Dead salmon litter the water. Belly up and shredded, the flow carries them towards the sea.

A bird speaks into the wind, chirrups sharp noises through the trees.

Clouds hang across the sky.

In the river, something from nothing. Life from death. Movement and meaning from two ancient halves, joined together, each passing on more than all the words of wit and sense could ever say.

In the river, the memory of love. Thin, small, tough. Waiting to be found. Always waiting. Always there.

And what of us, who cannot place our feet among that water?

Our water is here. And in it there is life.

And what of life?

Yours to live.

And what of love?

Yours to give.

The End

Printed in Great Britain
by Amazon